Published by
NineStar Press
PO Box 91792
Albuquerque, New Mexico, 87199
www.ninestarpress.com

Print ISBN #978-1-947139-26-8
Cover by Natasha Snow
Edited by Jason Bradley

To Angus and his humour,
Clinton for his support,
and Warren, without whom these tales wouldn't exist.

Adam is dead, but that's not his only problem. His husband, Wade, is still alive and sleeping with losers. His guardian angel, Guy, has grown fond of the liquor cabinet. And Adam suspects his demise was the result of foul play.

Meanwhile, in the depths of the Afterlife, the devil forces Adam to put on a play for the sinners. If he fails to entertain them, Guy's parents will spend eternity in the Underworld.

As he gambles with the freedom of the damned angels, Adam comes to terms with infidelity, friendship, and the reason why he was the victim of a double murder.

DRAMA QUEENS
and
Devilish Schemes

Actors and Angels, Book 3

Kevin Klehr

Chapter One

IT WAS LIKE being in a Hollywood remake of *The Jetsons*, suspended in air and surrounded by cloudless sky, with interweaving conveyor belts shifting us farther to the front.

Behind me a couple of lesbians fidgeted while peering forward, trying to see where we were going. Below, another mix of curious folk deliberately moved forward on this mechanical mess of pathways. Above me, the same.

"Do you have any idea what's going on?" asked one of the women behind me.

While she could pass for the girl next door, all made up with lips as red as a 1950s advert model, her checkered dress spoiled the effect with its huge smoldering burn mark.

"What happened," I queried.

Her partner stuck out what was left of her tongue. It too was charcoal black with a melted piercing smeared all over it.

"Let's just say, never get frisky outside while there's a thunderstorm."

She reached for her skirt and was about to lift it to prove her point. I clutched her wrist just in time.

"I get it. Your girlfriend's stud became the conductor. I don't need to see something that will haunt me for the rest of my life."

Her eyes widened. "*Your life*? Look at your chest!"

I released her arm and felt my heart. It was like someone had used too much starch while ironing my shirt. I examined a rusty brown stain on the crisp white cotton.

"I've returned, but this time for good," I muttered.

"Wha uw ya awing awout?" said the one with the brittle tongue.

"What did she say?"

"I think she wants to know what you're talking about."

I stood on tippy-toes to see farther ahead, but all I saw was a long row of people waiting patiently.

"I've been here before, I think. I'm not sure." I jumped high on the spot but still couldn't see where we were going. "I guess that's why I've got this frantic ink blot on my chest."

"Sweet cheeks, it's blood."

"Yes, I know that."

"So what's your story? How did it get there?"

I felt it again. Its sandpaper texture began to crumble. "I wish I knew." Bending sideways, I tried to steal a glimpse, but it was no use.

"Well, it's not quite how I imagined it. I'm not sure it's how you saw it either, Frida." She held her girlfriend's hand. "I was expecting tattooed angels parked on clouds with big black motorcycles ready to take us to Heaven."

Frida nodded.

"What did you expect, um, what's your name?"

"Adam."

"Hi, I'm Sue." We shook hands. "And this is Frida."

"Ice oo eet yoo."

"My pleasure."

"So, is this the way you pictured it?"

"No, I can't say it is. My partner isn't here."

"What's his name?"

"Wade. We've been together for nearly nineteen years. Or at least, we were."

"I'm sorry he's not with you."

I felt my bloodstain once more.

"Well, at least he survived, if what happened to me happened to him, if that makes sense?" I bit my bottom lip. "Actually I really don't know what I'm talking about."

"Aw leees ee awive..."

Sue raised her hand like a cop stopping traffic.

"Don't try to speak, darling. It looks like hard work."

"Yeah, but I get what Frida's trying to say. At least Wade's alive instead of here."

"A silver lining in the cloud."

"That's one way of looking at it."

Below me a young chap in a Second World War uniform peeled off his gloves. His conveyor belt had stopped. An African woman wearing more colors than a rainbow tried to speak to him, but he seemed too traumatized to reply. She raised her arms in disappointment and began talking to the gray-haired woman behind her.

"Leopard print," said Sue.

"Huh?"

"Check out the middle-aged woman in the leopard print, far behind us. Wow! She's wearing more jewelry than a 1960s movie star."

I looked. "I think she is a 60s movie star. Look at that beehive!"

"Jackie O she ain't."

"And look at the older woman next to her. A lollipop in a pantsuit."

"Adam, how can they be from the 60s?"

"Now I know I've been here before." I glanced ahead and saw the tip of a wing obstructed by the others on my conveyor belt. I couldn't hold back my smile. "Sue, let me ask you something. What era are you from?"

"Nineteen ninety-three. Why? Aren't you?"

I pointed to the man in uniform. Sue's jaw dropped steadily.

"And what country?"

"Poland. And you?"

"Australia, twenty-first century."

"You speak Polish well for an Australian."

"Sue, I'm not speaking Polish."

She shared stunned looks with Frida.

"Wha iz ee alking avout?"

"Girls, you're about to enter a world I've been dreaming of returning to since I was last taken from earth before my time."

"Maybe you should *try* Polish. I have no idea what you mean."

Frida rotated her finger by the side of her head; a gesture to make out I was loony. Sue shrugged before carrying on a private conversation with her girlfriend about the family they'd left behind.

A few drops of water splashed on my face. I looked to the moving path above. A group of teenagers also from the 60s flower-power days stood shivering, saturated to the core. One long-haired guy, with enough swirls on his shirt to send you into a trance, saw me.

"Never do your own plumbing when you're tripping, man," he called. "I flooded the apartment."

"Why didn't you run outside?"

A naked girl with waist-length long hair clutched onto his arm. "I thought I was swimming in candy floss," she replied.

"Candy floss!" he said. "I thought the sky had fallen and there was no escape."

"Weren't we in space, floating?" asked another.

I chuckled before bending sideways to look ahead. I saw half his body. My guardian angel, Guy. He acknowledged me with a kind grin. I was eager to jump to the head of the queue. I took a calm breath, stood up straight, and closed my eyes.

I already sensed his comforting hugs, letting me know I'd returned to safety. I could feel his strong wings wrap around me like an extra layer of armor. Nothing would harm me here in the Afterlife, not with him by my side.

"Adam's here," said another voice I recognized.

"Yeah," Guy replied. "There's something I need to explain."

"Mannix?" I mumbled to myself.

Many passengers later I was at the front. I stepped off the conveyor belt onto thin air, and before a word was uttered, both the angel and my old friend wrapped their arms around me. I clutched them tightly, never wanting to let go. Huge smiles engulfed us all. Behind me were bewildered murmurs, as a stray tear from Guy softened my cheek.

"I've missed you," I said to my angel. I kissed him tenderly on the forehead. "And I missed you too, Mannix."

"Welcome to the Afterlife again," said Guy.

"Why am I here?" I whispered. We stepped apart.

"I think this time you're actually dead," Mannix replied.

He sounded unsure, like a wife telling her tired husband that there might be a burglar in their house. He was still in his early thirties, just as he was the last time I was whisked off to the Afterlife six months earlier.

His sensual demeanor still warmed me in places I'm too polite to mention, even though his boyhood looks had faded slightly since we last met. A man was taking his place. A man wise beyond his years, wearing older-sexy like a stylish coat.

"Where's Wade?" I asked.

"Sadly mourning your demise, my friend," Guy said in a hushed tone. "Adam, we'll talk about that later."

I touched the dried blood on my shirt, crumbling it into tiny pieces that fell away.

"Guy, I need to know what happened."

He turned to Mannix. "I'm releasing you from welcoming duties to show Adam his new home."

"Which is where?" the young man asked.

Guy pulled out a key from his trouser pocket. "The apartment under mine." He had a devilish grin. "Adam's not the only one who needs a friend at the moment."

"So you and Guy welcome the dead?" I asked.

"Yeah, but we call them new visitors," Mannix replied. He sipped his scotch and Coke. "*I've* just started, but Guy's been doing it for ages. He got a promotion when they put in the new conveyor belts. They needed to upgrade." He looked around the room before leaning toward me. "Too many lost souls coming at once."

I had showered and changed, and was now sitting with Mannix at a lavish bar called the Carousel in the Medieval Quarter. Two drunken men in full armor jousted with plastic toy swords in the corner while a topless woman with tassels on her perfect breasts attempted to tango as she ignored their clatter. Some drinkers shared their attention between the drunks and the playful dancer, pointing and chatting as if they considered themselves boring by comparison. But to me, they were just as fascinating.

The last time I'd visited the Afterlife, I was still alive, because Guy felt the need to take me away from my earthly dramas. And once again, the supporting extras still intrigued me in this land of the dead. After all, this part of the Medieval Quarter was known as the Carnival of Lost Souls. A fitting description.

"There's something bothering me, Mannix."

"Besides not knowing how you died."

"Well, there's that, but..."

One of the armored men collapsed to the ground with a thud. A tall woman in a lime backless dress stood up and applauded. I clapped briefly before I realized that no one else was taking her lead. A barman strolled over to check on him.

"Adam, you were saying?"

"My new apartment looks a lot like mine and Wade's back in Sydney."

"We do that. I know it's unsettling at first, but it helps new arrivals fit in."

"But how did you do it? The couch is the same. My stereo is the same, just without the television. The kitchen is kind of the same, just in a lighter color."

"Adam, this is the Afterlife. We're masters of pulling things from thin air."

"But doesn't it seem odd to you?"

"I've had more time to get used to it."

"This whole place, it's like an ethereal version of Earth. There's running water. Electricity. Music collections. Food and alcohol." The waiter came to refill my glass of merlot. "But you know what, Mannix? I've never seen a toilet. Come to think of it, I didn't need one the last time I was here." The waiter nodded before going back to the bar. "And besides that, the only thing that points to this place being the Afterlife is a bunch of people hanging around bars in period costume from a hell of a lot of eras. And, of course, there's an angel. Take that away and we may as well still be alive."

"Maybe your wine is the blood of Christ?"

"Don't go there, Mannix. If it was, I'd be more enlightened."

An assortment of bizarre collectibles adorned small shelves on the walls. Some looked like rejects from a charity shop. Other's seemed too precious to be gathering dust. A detailed figurine of a girl walking her shih tzu sat next to a clay horse's head, so lifelike it seemed more a freaky attempt at taxidermy.

Each table also had an ornament sitting on it. Ours was a vintage doll with a wonky eye. I picked it up while watching a fiendish man in a leather jacket striding up to the topless woman.

"Mannix, is Guy still with that boyfriend of his?"

"You mean Joshua? What made you think of him?"

I pointed to the man who was now trying to touch the woman's tassel. She took his delinquent hand and slapped it.

"I see your point, Adam. He reminds me of Joshua too."

"Yes, with the same personality it seems."

As if written as their cue in a play, Guy and Joshua entered the Carousel that very moment. Joshua was in his angel disguise, with a slight emo twist highlighted by black feathered wings. When he was his demon self, the wings were still black, but resembled those on a bat. Small horns were also part of his natural look, but when he slummed it in the Afterlife, he couldn't get away with being himself. The only clue to his true form could be found in his reflection, as I discovered when catching a glimpse of his likeness in a drinking glass.

They headed for the bar, Josh gazing at me briefly as if I was the only witness to a murder he'd committed.

"Mannix, what does that beautiful angel see in that sarcastic demon? And why is an angel going out with a demon?"

"Between you and me, I think it has less to do with romance and more to do with the fact that Joshua knows where Guy's parents are."

"Oh yes, I forgot about that. Guy never met his folks. Something about being brought up by a fortune-teller, wasn't it?"

"Shh. They're almost here."

Guy plonked a large champagne bottle on our table before Joshua landed four glasses next to it.

"It's not peer pressure. It's peer support," he said. His black wings fluttered.

"I'll drink to that," Guy replied. They both sat. "So, Adam, how do you like your new flat?"

"It's spooking me out."

"From memory, everything spooks you out," replied Joshua.

"Only when it has dark wings and a 'try hard' attitude."

"Now, now, boys," Guy said. He popped the cork and began to pour. "I don't want my two favorite men—"

Mannix faked a cough.

"Sorry, three favorite men bickering. I need to celebrate!"

He slid my drink toward me.

"What's the deal with that cock-eyed doll you're holding?" Joshua asked.

I looked at the toy's face. "I forgot it was still in my hand."

"You've been using it to punctuate your gestures ever since you picked it up," said Mannix.

"It must be my security blanket."

"Don't worry," said Guy. "A few celebratory drinks will ease your nerves." As the champagne reached his mouth, his glass became wobbly.

"Are you already drunk?" Mannix asked.

"I just had one drink before I came."

Joshua peered down his nose.

"Okay, maybe two."

Joshua's eyes now looked to the ceiling.

"No seriously, only two."

I gazed at Mannix who nodded discreetly. I then peered at Joshua who seemed to have trouble smiling.

"Why did you start without us?" I asked.

"I want to celebrate your arrival," Guy replied. "After all, Adam, I've missed you." He raised his glass. "To an old friend becoming my neighbor."

We clinked, then sipped.

"Now that the formalities are over, can you please tell me how I died? That was a nasty bloodstain on my shirt."

"In time, Adam. I need to ask for a favor, first."

"You need *my* help this time? Of course, my angel buddy. What is it?"

He looked to his lover.

"Guy is going to meet his parents," Joshua replied.

"And I need moral support."

I reached for his hand. He grasped mine gently.

"Wow. I'd consider it an honor to stand by your side, old friend. Where are they?"

Again he looked to Joshua.

"That's a secret for now," Joshua replied.

"Why?"

The black-winged immortal shook his head so only I would see.

"He won't tell me," said Guy.

"Adam, I suggested you should be here when he meets them," Joshua replied. "I know how much he respects you."

I glanced at Mannix.

"He said the same thing to me," he declared. "For whatever reason, Joshua wanted you to be here to support Guy."

"But Guy has both you and Joshua. Why wait till I died? Are you recruiting an ensemble cast for the reunion?"

"It's difficult to explain," said Joshua. "The more friends he has here, the better."

Guy let go of my hand and topped up his champagne, then drank. He put the glass down, unsteadily. I picked up the doll and stared at its imperfect face.

"Wow, I just arrive and already there's mystery and adventure. I need Wade by my side to share it with. I'm missing him terribly. I just wish I knew how I died."

"Adam's right, Guy," said Mannix. "I think he needs to know what happened."

"The secrecy is killing me. Oh wait, I'm already dead. Okay, the secrecy is driving me mad."

"All right," Guy answered. "I'll take you to see Wade. That's all I can do for the moment."

"Can't you also tell me how my shirt got covered in blood?"

"No, I can't." He reached for *my* hand this time. I put down the doll and clasped his soft palm. "You have to work out what happened for yourself, Adam. It will start coming to you. That's the way things work here." He clasped tighter, but somehow I suspected he didn't actually know himself. "But I guess if I take you to see Wade, your healing process will begin."

"My healing process! Shouldn't I know how I died first? Why don't you tell me before we see Wade?"

"Now that you're here, you need to take one step at a time. Come to terms with your demise, calmly. If I tell you everything up front, you might find it too hard to handle."

I sighed.

"I know this is hard to take in, Adam," Mannix said, "but Guy's right. I've made the mistake of telling someone too much too soon. It wasn't pretty."

"What happened?" I asked.

"A loving parent was poisoned by his kids for the inheritance money. Years of therapy followed here in the Afterlife."

"Oh dear. I wasn't murdered, was I?"

"Trust your guardian angel. Let him guide you."

Guy stood, and as we were still holding hands, I too was lifted from my chair.

"Adam, it's time to start healing," he said. "Let's see Wade."

Chapter Two

"CAN HE SEE us?" I asked.

"No, Adam, he can't see us at all."

We were standing in my old bedroom where Wade was checking something in the wardrobe. I was still holding hands with Guy, and he made sure we took our champagne glasses with us.

"Can he hear us?"

"He has no knowledge of our presence."

"What's that man doing in our bed?"

I took a huge swig of my drink. This good-looking bearded dude huddled under the duvet, watching Wade check the closet.

"Seriously," Wade said to his companion, "there's no one here."

"Check under the bed," replied the stranger.

"You're joking, aren't you?"

"No, it's just a ritual I need you to go through."

"This isn't part of some kinky fantasy, is it?"

"No, Wade. I do this every night."

"For goodness sake, why?"

"I don't want to be attacked if I fall asleep."

"Jerry, you've just met me for the first time tonight. How do you know *I'm* not going to attack you?"

His one-night stand didn't answer. He simply quivered under the covers.

"Guy, what on earth is going on?"

"Wade is getting sex."

"Thanks for pointing out the obvious, but why is he looking for sex? I've just died, for goodness sake!"

My guardian angel wobbled slightly before letting go of my hand and steadying himself on my shoulder. Jerry opened the bedside drawer.

"What are you looking for?" Wade asked.

"A knife. A gun. An axe."

"Why don't I just get into bed with you so you can stop this silly nonsense?"

"I don't know. You've got me thinking about this murderer thing. Have you killed anyone?"

My husband sighed. I felt my chest where the bloodstain once was.

"Guy, he didn't? No, not my Wade. I've known him for nearly nineteen years and…" My celestial friend stayed poker-faced. Not even his eyes, of which the whites resembled mini roadmaps, gave anything away. "Come to think of it, Wade has a fascination with horror films."

"Adam, stop overthinking. Just watch and learn."

That man in our bed leisurely pulled down the duvet. He was unusually thin. I could've picked him up by the neck on laundry day and used him as a clothes-peg.

"Guy, do I really need to watch this?"

Wade moved toward him with the grace of a first-time actor in a porn film. As Jerry lay back, spreading his legs, I had a mad urge to pull on his foot and make a wish. My partner climbed on board, nestling his forehead into Nervous Nelly's beard.

"Your husband's got technique, Adam."

"Yes, I know, but do we really have to stay?"

"You want answers, don't you?" He stepped closer to the bed. "And there's a lot to learn here."

"Guy, you're drunk, and quite frankly, you look like you want to join in."

He gave me a sheepish grin.

"Guy!"

Jerry whined like a mother hyena who'd misplaced her kids.

"Adam, trust me. This is where your healing begins."

"I hope you're getting your kicks from watching this, because I'm definitely not."

"I'm getting 'lovemaking' tips."

Wade opened his mouth, sliding it onto his lover's. Soon they were at it like two teenagers with their braces caught.

"I didn't know kissing could look so unattractive," I said.

"Wow. Wade's very sensual."

"Guy, can I upsize your voyeurism with a side of fries?"

"Relax. Don't forget I'm your guardian angel. I've seen you and Wade at it plenty of times."

He hiccupped, covering his mouth. I swigged the rest of my champagne.

"Roar," groaned Jerry. "Let me do something to you that you'll never forget, Wayne."

"It's Wade."

"Huh?"

"My name's Wade."

"Let me do something you'll never forget, Wade."

Jerry started licking my husband's armpit like a dribbling mutt. My man moaned in gratitude.

"I never realized Wade was into saliva." Guy shrugged while peering right into the wet underarm action. "Come to think of it, I never realized he was into thin bearded men."

"What was that?" asked Jerry. His slobbering came to a halt.

"What was what?" asked Wade.

"That noise?"

"What noise?"

"Wade, go and check downstairs."

My old man looked hesitant, but this thing he'd brought home looked at him with puppy-dog eyes. Wade left the bed and wandered down the hall. Guy and I followed. He marched around the living room before trudging to the bathroom, making enough noise for lover boy to hear from our room. He opened the cupboard and reached for a prescription box of tablets I'd never seen before. He popped two pills and quickly followed them with a gulp of tap water from the palm of his hand.

"Oh, Adam, why did you leave me like this?"

I looked over his shoulder and read the packet. Valium. Wade was hooked on valium!

"Guy, what's going on? Why is he taking those pills?"

But my angel guide gestured toward Wade.

"Why did our relationship have to end like this?" my beautiful man said.

"Wade, I love you, but what are you talking about?"

I knew he couldn't hear me, but maybe in his thoughts I could get through. He leaned against the basin, staring blankly.

"You left me, Adam, long before our time." A tear trickled. "What am I saying? Your spirit had left me long before you ever did."

"Guy, I need to know what he's talking about."

"Adam, I really can't tell you. Not yet."

My angel's words were slurred, but his mood was sober.

"Why can't you tell me? Wade's in pain. Did I do something?"

"If you were still here, Adam," Wade moaned, "we could talk about your feelings. Why you went and did the things you did. Now I just have to live with unfinished business."

Wade sighed in a groggy fashion. He didn't hurry back to the saliva queen. As I looked to Guy for some kind of relief from seeing my lost lover in torment, my lost lover buried his head in his hands and sobbed quietly.

Chapter Three

LATER I WAS back in the Afterlife, sitting alone in my apartment. Outside it was autumnal. Trees stood naked as if their spirits had drifted in search of a friendlier season. Flowers kept to themselves, too cold to show their glory. I wanted to hibernate with them, within my walls.

There wasn't a chance I could leave this god-awful place and breathe real air again; to live among the living. I wanted to shower with Wade, soap his back, dry his body, and kiss away all his pain. I'd then make love to him as if nothing mattered.

There was a knock on the door. I didn't answer. Guy let himself in.

"Wasn't my door locked?" I asked.

He wiggled his wings several times before he looked nauseous. "Oh dear." He put his hand to his mouth. "That fluttering wing thing I was struggling to do was me trying to say that your door was locked, but I'm an angel. I can pretty much go anywhere."

"You look like something the cat dragged in."

"I tried to have a nap but tossed and turned instead. I wouldn't be a good guardian if I didn't come back and help you through this."

"I'm not sure you're a good guardian now. Visiting Wade was hard. Why did you do that to me?"

Guy rested his palms on his temples and collapsed into an armchair. "I had to start somewhere, Adam." His head drooped "I know it was hard. But no pain, no gain."

"I don't want catchphrases. You're supposed to be my friend. I mean, the last time I was here, you really helped. But you're being all secretive about how I got here. Why can't I remember?"

"You're not alone. Everyone who comes here doesn't remember how they died. It's too traumatic for them to deal with right away." He met my gaze with a soft smile. "If our new arrivals knew every detail of how they died, then we'd be spending all our time passing out boxes of tissues."

"Then pass me the tissues. I need to know."

He leaned toward me, but I crossed my arms in anger.

"Adam, think about this. If you knew, what would it solve? It's another layer of hurt you'd need to push through. But Wade's missing you. That's the hurt you need to deal with before anything else."

"Then let me talk to him!"

"I can't! You're dead!" Guy shut his eyes. "I'm sorry, Adam. I didn't mean to shout. I go through this every day with our grieving newcomers. And trust me, they grieve just as much on this side as they do back on Earth. And if I could take their pain away the moment they arrived, I would. But what would that achieve? Lost souls in ignorant bliss, caught in a moment devoid of reality. Even an angel has his orders. I can only do so much."

I sat silent. Somewhere my partner in life was suffering and I'd abandoned him. For the first time in the better part of two decades, we were no longer a team. Yet both of us felt each other's absence like a deep wound.

"Guy, I'm sorry." I shook my head. "Okay, I get it, I'm dead. But it hurts. I had the perfect life and now I'm here, and from what I can piece together from the small amount of evidence I've gotten, I died through no fault of my own."

"Yes, Adam, that's right. But don't make that your starting point."

I tilted my head back, wanting to scream.

"No, hear me out. You heard Wade's grief asking why you did the things you did. Your memory will gradually return, and I'm here to help you deal with it."

I stared at him like an emotionless zombie.

"I love you, Adam. I chose to be your guardian angel because you're a gentle soul. And here and now, I need that gentle soul to be my friend."

He offered his hand. I shook it begrudgingly.

"Can I do anything for Wade while I'm here?"

Guy stood, releasing my grip. "I'll be right back."

He tottered out my door like a personal assistant about to search for an important file. When he returned, he had a joint in one hand and a lighter in the other.

"No, that's not what I need right now."

"It'll dull the pain."

I considered it before shaking my head. He laid the gifts on the coffee table. I stared at them, slightly tempted.

"Go on," said another voice. Joshua had entered the room. "It's been rolled from a plant in my secret garden. Trust me, one puff and it will be like a kaleidoscope of all your favorite television shows back on Earth."

"Why are you being nice to me, demon?"

His bat wings raised him an inch from the ground and landed him next to my chair.

"And why are you here?"

"I asked him here to help me cheer you up," Guy answered.

"But you were only gone for a minute."

"I was invited about an hour ago," Joshua replied. "I made myself comfortable upstairs waiting for Guy to get back."

"Look, I appreciate you both being here, I guess. No, let's get real here. I appreciate Guy being here, but as for you, Josh, I'm not sure."

"Darling, I can be a great help too. I've seen it all, done it all, and been responsible for it all…" His finger rested on his chin. "Oh who am I kidding? I'm here for the weed."

"Joshua!" his boyfriend cried.

"Okay, I'm here for Adam as well. He's the most entertaining human I've met. He can amuse me for hours, even when he doesn't know I'm watching."

"Look, I don't care if you smoke weed," I said. "But please, not here and now. Go back to Guy's place."

"He doesn't want us, lover. He wants to wallow in his own tears rather than dance to our tune."

"I'm sorry, Adam," Guy said. "We'll leave you in peace."

As they reached the door, something inside made me call out to them.

"Oh, what is it now?" the demon asked.

"Um, I don't really want to be alone."

Guy rushed to my side.

"And if it means I have to have both of you here, then I'll man up and deal with it."

"Adam's more confused than a mood ring on a manic-depressive."

"Joshua, let's change the subject," said Guy.

"Good idea," I replied. "Sit down, both of you. But please, save the weed till later. I just want to talk about something other than Wade."

"Are you sure?" Guy asked.

"Yeah. If I smoke now, I might get paranoid and freak out over what happened."

Joshua casually made his way to the two-seater. Guy joined him.

"Let's talk about..." I looked out the window.

In the distance, a woman tossed a ball to her toddler. He clapped his hands and jumped in the air, ignoring the ball. A small girl dressed in a cape, as if walking to grandma's with a basket of goods, stopped, picked up the ball, and gave it back to the mother.

"Adam, we haven't got all day," Joshua said.

"Let's talk about Guy's parents. I remember that you said you never met your parents and that you, Joshua, know where they are."

"Got it in one, Earth Boy."

"So where are they?"

The demon pursed his lips.

"He won't tell me," Guy replied.

"It's complicated," said Joshua.

"Ah, so I'm not the only one subjected to secrets."

Guy's fluttered his wings thrice.

"Okay, if I remember correctly, an aunt raised you."

"Auntie Jemima. A woman in love with life, although I didn't give her enough credit at the time."

"How come?"

Joshua laid a hand on Guy's knee.

"I think that when you're separated from your parents, and you know it, it makes you feel less special. After all, you need your parents to teach you to fly. Give you your independence. Make you feel free."

"She didn't teach you?"

"She couldn't. You see, she wasn't my real auntie. Just someone who raised me after I was abandoned long before I could remember."

"I still don't get why she didn't teach you to fly."

"She *wasn't* an angel. I was almost a teenager when I realized she physically couldn't be related to me."

"But you would have worked that out long before your teenage years."

He placed his hand on Joshua's.

"That's the thing. As a kid, I sort of knew but didn't want to know."

"How awful."

"More awkward than awful. Especially in my teenage years. You know what they're like. Every emotion is amplified." He exchanged glances with his lover. "I eventually used Aunt Jem's lack of wings as a reason to be rebellious."

I stared outside again, pondering why Guy had parents. *Didn't God simply create angels?* Clouds were parting in the sky, adding light to the street scene. The toddler was jumping around even more now, as if a sugar hit had taken hold.

"Wasn't there someone around to teach you to fly?" I asked.

Guy moved his hand away from Joshua's.

"I tried to teach him to fly when we were teenagers," the demon said. "I had more faith in him than he had in himself."

"Nice one, Josh. Civil conversation with me. You should do this more often."

He poked his tongue out.

"I wish I'd shared your faith in me at the time," Guy confessed. "I took out my low self-esteem on my Aunt Jem. Keeping my distance from her. Hardly eating. She tried her best to cheer me up, but I felt way too sorry for myself. I was a flightless loser."

"Well, you almost flew when we were teenagers," Joshua avowed.

"Does that mean you still can't fly?" I asked.

"Oh I can fly," he said. "Many years later, I befriended someone who popped into the Afterlife for the short term. He made it his unofficial mission to teach me." He lowered his head.

"So where are Guy's parents, Josh?"

The demon looked at the ceiling. "I can't say."

"Oh come on, Joshy. At the Carousel you said you were waiting for me to get here to support our friend's quest for his parents. I can't believe you're keeping something like that from him. And for this long!"

"Trust me. I can't tell you yet."

"Your boyfriend was drunk when I got here. Now he's hungover, but he still brought over a joint. This is not the Guy I remember. What have you done to him?"

"I'm a good boyfriend."

"Really, Josh? Really? What does a demon know about fragility?"

The spineless lover stood. "I'm a better friend to him than you'll ever be."

My guardian angel also stood. "Joshua!" he screeched. "You are addressing Adam, my friend. You were waiting until he got here to go fetch my parents. Now you're changing the rules."

"I am not changing the rules, dear boyfriend." Joshua's tone was measured. "But some things need to wait. That's what *you* tell the newly dead all the time."

"Yes, and the newly dead have enough to deal with, without your sarcastic tone added to their real life dramas!" Guy's booming voice made my apartment shake. "But in the end, I guess a leopard can't change his spots."

"And what's that supposed to mean, you alcoholic do-gooder?"

"Maybe both of you should stop," I said. "Before things start being thrown."

"Oh, Adam, darling," Joshua sniped, "we're just acting like human beings. I'm sure you're used to seeing that."

"So, I'm an alcoholic do-gooder, am I? And what kind of demon are you? One who hides himself in this world disguised as a trampy cherub? You're hardly cupid, you know."

"Heavenly friends, let's calm down," I muttered, but my words got caught in my throat. "I mean really; I don't want lightning bolts ripping past me."

"I wear that angel disguise so I don't freak out your precious dead folk. Give me some credit!"

"Oh, is that it, Joshua? You can't just be yourself?"

"Oh please. This troop of halfwits you have to help out are only here because they're the unstable lot. The failures. The duds." He pointed at me. "And if you can't see these losers are what's keeping you on their level, then maybe I made a big mistake."

"Josh, watch where you point," I mumbled. "I don't want to be turned into anything slimy."

"And that's your whole problem, lover," Guy replied. He stood beside me. "You have no soul. You're a dark demon. Devoid of empathy."

"You are so fried half the time that you hit out at the people who actually care."

I shuddered at his vicious voice.

"Can you blame me? You know where my parents are and you won't tell me! Of course I'm a wreck. And I've got the dispossessed to deal on top of your secrecy."

I picked up the joint from the coffee table. "Ah, *that's* what we need," I said. "Mother's little helper. Who wants to light it?"

"And your precious dispossessed are your life, Guy. Not me. Not my needs. Not my love." The demon turned toward my front door like an aging actress about to make a dignified exit. "And for some misguided reason, I thought we were right for each other." He walked out, never looking back.

"I'm so sorry," I said.

Guy wiped the corner of his eye, then snatched the joint from my hand. As it hit his lips, it sparked with a crimson flame.

"I never got to have sex with him," he suddenly blurted while half smiling, as smoke blew in my direction.

Chapter Four

GUY SPUN LIKE a whirling dervish in slow motion to a dance beat in the background, while his wings flailed like a mad woman arguing with the world. Soon he was bouncing on the spot, summoning the ghost of a witch doctor casting an evil spell on his ex-lover. And all through this crazed dance was a little boy "so close" at finding his lost youth.

I too was dazed and stoned, staring out the window, searching for answers that I knew weren't there. The emotionless trees whispered in the night air. They were in control of this landscape as there was no one in sight. Humans had been painted out of the picture, insignificant to a backdrop that existed only for my angel and me.

"Do you like this track, Adam?"

"Well, it's keeping us upbeat. Isn't that why you put it on?"

"I'm in disco paradise! Come dance with me."

"Guy, don't get me wrong. I like it. It's just a little, um..." He stopped his one-man show. "It's just a little camp. Last time I was here, you played sixties psychedelia. Hey, we're off our faces. That's what we should be listening to."

"I don't need to trip on my morbid thoughts, Adam. I need good vibes. I need release."

I rummaged through the record collection. A colorful assortment of snazzy artwork eased past my fingertips. Seventies divas with attitude posed next to frizzy-haired backup singers. Silver balls and neon lights ignited dancers in loose toffee-toned clothing. Two young men in safari suits stood next to a woman wearing ferns. They were in the wrong hunting party.

But then I was welcomed by sophisticated funksters in mod attire. I had found the acid jazz section.

"Let me get our groove on." I pulled the vinyl from its sleeve. "Here we go. Jamiroquai. It's music to keep coming back to."

Guy extended his waving fingers, as if trying to hypnotize me. I peered into his sneaky eyes and grinned. Soon his ass found its swing and his body followed. I boogied up to him, matching his rhythm.

"Why do you get stoned so often?" I shouted over the music.

"So I feel like I'm in a Baz Luhrmann film."

"But why the escape?"

"Angels need to find themselves as much as mortals."

"Wow. So this is your escape?"

"Confidence is a hard won mistress."

"But Guy, you can't crumble. You're my rock."

He grabbed my wrist and swung me around. The ambient light sparked my creativity. I looked to him as my own playboy millionaire. His crystal-blue eyes and imaginary dark suit made me melt, as they had done for so many other bachelor hopefuls. But now I was his, and his alone. His private jet had been chartered just so he could visit my ordinary life. His butler had treated us to French champagne. I put down my glass as I sprung back into his arms, but he quickly threw me to the wind.

My apartment disappeared to make way for an army of tango dancers. Their mass of frenzied feet drowned the music. Rat-a-tat-tat! One man with a blond curl caught my eye as he spun past with his partner. I swayed until my lover whisked me back, twirling like a goddess in flamenco heels.

He was warm. Hot, in fact. His wings engulfed me. A historic building in a rosy hue shimmered behind him. Errant heels echoed down the streets. I swooned as his face turned into the latte-skinned man I had left in the mortal world.

I jolted out of his arms.

"What's the matter, Adam?"

My apartment returned in a flash.

"You were Wade." I turned down the stereo and collapsed onto the lounge. "Oh, Guy. I'm missing him."

Guy sat next to me. "Look at us," he said. "We're two tragic romantics."

"But your man is still in this world. Mine is a lifetime away."

"Adam, I can't go back to Joshua."

My jaw dropped.

"No, hear me out. We've had no sex because he says he wants to wait.

And he's been playing with my mind about my parents. I can't take anymore."

"He's a demon, Guy. Was it a good choice to begin with? Even if he does know where your parents are, can you trust him?"

"I know he knows something that he's keeping from me. He waited for you to get here to give me support."

"But what if I died when I was older and not in my forties? You'd have a long wait."

"I would have brought you to this point in time."

"Oh yeah. There are advantages to being an angel."

There was a loud clanking sound coming from outside. A horde of medieval soldiers marched down the street. Behind them, a small blonde girl frolicked in a tutu and a necklace of flowers, as if she was declaring the arrival of spring.

"I swear this place gets nuttier every time I visit," I said.

"One of them is Tyson from the apartment next to mine. It's the night of the Harlequin Dance at the Carnival of Lost Souls."

"Of course it is. And they're off to fight a metal dragon that shoots aluminum foil from its nostrils. And that little girl is really a femme fatale in disguise who just needs something to wrap her husband's body in so it won't go off in the fridge while she's waiting for a quiet night so no witnesses see her dispose of him in the muddy creek frequented by the neighborhood's teenage lovers. It all makes perfect sense. This whole place is the theater of the absurd!"

"You're missing Wade, aren't you?"

I nodded. "And I'm starting to feel something went terribly wrong in our final days. Well, besides the fact that I had blood on my shirt. My mood since I've been here has been a deep shade of melancholy, although I've tried to hide it."

"What do you think happened?"

"You're not going to tell me, are you, Guy?"

A second team of armored men made their way past our building. They were followed by a shirtless dude with a chest as hard as iron. His gold turban and loose pants were in need of a flying carpet. I shook my head in amusement.

"Adam, what do you think happened in your final days?"

"There are men. Or there's another man. I think. He's striking. Brooding, almost." I tilted back my head. "Is it someone I'm jealous of?"

"Think about it, Adam. Concentrate."

I closed my eyes. "I know the feelings but can't see a vision. There is a man, I'm sure. He's giving me a sense of understanding. But is it Wade who's making me feel settled, or the man?"

"Maybe they both do in their own way?"

I peered at Guy through one eye. "Guy, how did Joshua make you feel?"

"Why are you changing the subject?"

"Curiosity."

His wings fluttered briefly. "At first, annoyed. We were like two alien beings from different planets. But then he became gentler in his approach."

I snickered, not meaning to.

"Yes I know he's blunt, but you don't see him like I do."

"Guy, come on. Mr. Charming he ain't."

He raised an eyebrow.

"Sorry. It's your story. I'll shut up."

"As I was saying, there is something sexy about him. And beneath that façade of sarcastic wit, there's a sensitive soul." He turned to me, grinning, but soon lost his smile. "Seriously, Adam, he *is* sensitive."

"I didn't say he wasn't."

"I know. But it's that look you just had on your face."

"What look?"

"Like a parent listening to their son telling them he's got a crush on his teacher."

My jaw dropped.

"Adam, I know you better than you think."

"Guy, light that joint again. You might not like what I'm about to say."

Chapter Five

I CHICKENED OUT in expressing my opinion to Guy. Well, at least for the moment. I encouraged him to take me to the Harlequin Dance instead.

Three tall jokers frolicked with their faces painted white. A club symbol, usually found on a deck of cards, decorated one of the men's cheeks. Another man had a spade while the last had a heart.

A woman, sporting a snug bodysuit with black and yellow stripes, buzzed around us, wiggling her stinging tail. A man with camp spirit straddled her lethal tip, laughing as if he'd just heard a clever joke.

Somewhere a piano accordion played. Elsewhere a mandolin was stroked. A whirling blaze of rainbow hues and fragrances weaved by me and through me. I shook my tush as Guy moved his wings as part of his own inspired dance.

"I wasn't this stoned when we left your place," I said.

"Adam, this is called being high on life."

"But I'm dead."

"But your soul is living!"

The armored men also joined in rhythm, clanking at the same time. Their clumsy attire made them stumble. Their rusted headwear screeched as they opened their visors to drink glasses of ale. And all the while, women avoided their boyhood bond.

Yet somehow, their friendly jeers made them safe in their own company. Their manhood was merely an expression borrowed for the night. But in the morning their testosterone would be locked up again in safety deposit boxes until next year.

"Guy, I'm not dressed for this. Everyone's in costume."

A little boy whisked past in a red go-cart, startling me. I wrapped my arms around my angel for comfort. His wings were gone.

"Do you like our outfits, Adam?"

Diamond shapes in cobalt and pale blue covered my arms. As I shook my head, I felt the droopy extensions of my hat bounce. I was a harlequin.

"Yes, I like it. It's pretty neat. And, Guy, you're not an angel anymore."

"I'm in disguise." His jester outfit was subtly highlighted by different shades of white.

"Did you tuck your wings somewhere the way drag queens tuck their...?"

"Tonight with you, Adam, I'm a man. A mortal, if you like. And I'd like to talk man to man about Joshua."

A smoky mist drifted through the crowd. A harp accompanied an ethereal female voice. But with all this sensory overload, all I could see were my angel's arresting eyes.

"Guy, how do I put this?"

"Just say it."

"I don't think he's right for you, whether he knows your parents or not."

"But it's nice having someone around."

"My dear guardian, even you should know there's nothing lonelier than a relationship that isn't working."

Behind him the fog drifted apart like a theater curtain. A small anime girl was in its place. Her vocals became one with the harp.

"Joshua can be kind, Adam."

"Really? Is it when he's sleeping?"

Guy smiled with affection. "He kisses in a way that keeps me warm."

"Anyone can kiss you that way. But is that enough of a reason to be a nervous pot-smoking drunk?"

He giggled before melding his lips with mine. This messenger of love didn't use his tongue. He didn't need to. Inside I felt like a superhero. Untouchable. Open to those in need.

His slender fingers tickled the back of my shaven skull, as my hands leisurely explored his well-formed back. We were dreamers heading down a road of miscalculated adventures.

But then he rubbed his nose against mine, arousing parts of me that an angel shouldn't toy with. My mouth tingled for more of this divine addiction as that Japanese song whispered in my ear.

Why am I flirting with my guardian angel? Am I missing Wade? Am I stoned or just making the best of being dead?

Guy moaned softly. His voice in harmony with the Asian girl. But the harp begged for attention through its mystical sighs, until the female voice screeched. Our embrace was murdered by manga.

"Why did you stop?" my harlequin man asked.

"I'll explain shortly," I replied. I looked around. No mist. No anime girl. No harp. "But I have a point to make, first."

He stood serenely. His eyes fixated on mine.

"And what is that point, Adam?"

"Was it as good for you as it was for me?"

He smirked.

"That proves my point. Anyone can kiss you and make you feel the way Joshua does. But how does he make you feel the rest of the time?"

"Confused. Stroppy. Annoyed. But on the other hand, kind of special."

"And that can sound like real love. Maybe it is. But, Guy, you have to sort out the confused, stroppy, and annoyed. Otherwise you'll become a lesser version of yourself." I held his hand. "Now, when does he make you feel these bad emotions?"

"Sometimes he says things that make me feel invisible."

"Like what?"

He looked to the ground. "Joshua snuck into my bed the other night. I stirred, trying not to become fully awake, but he kissed me on the cheek. I lurched at him, tasting his mouth. Soon we were at it, kissing. The sheets were thrown from the bed. Pillows scattered. You get the picture."

"That doesn't sound like you're invisible."

"But then he stopped. No explanation. No sex. He gave short answers when I questioned him."

"What did you ask?"

"I asked why he stopped. He said he wasn't up to it. I checked him downstairs. He was up for it." My wicked guardian grinned. "I asked why we couldn't take it further. He said he was tired. I jumped on him, wanting to ride him. But he was snoring." Guy's alluring eyes shared their sorrow. "I stayed awake for ages, just lying next to him."

"How can someone that looks like he invented original sin be so frigid? I mean, whether he's disguised as an angel or slumming it as a demon, he's hot!"

"Maybe it's me? Maybe he's not that into me?"

"Then why stay with him, Guy?"

"Because he knows where my parents are."

"So keep him as a friend. He's keeping your motor running but isn't ready to take you for a drive. Pop him in the garage and find someone better."

"Perhaps, Adam, I've just found someone better."

"Me?"

He nodded.

"Guy, you believe in the love Wade and I share, more than anyone I know. So why did you make a move on me?"

"You didn't resist."

"That's not what I asked."

"Perhaps I gave in to mortal tendencies."

"Then can I please have my angel back. He makes more sense than us stupid humans."

We stood as ourselves out of costume amongst the mayhem.

"So, Adam, what made you break our embrace?"

"That singer's voice reminded me of an ear-piercing scream." I rubbed my chin. "Do you know the voice I mean? She was a little Japanese lass here a moment ago."

"The soundtrack to our kiss. Yes, I heard it." He pointed to her in the distance.

I had to raise myself on tippy-toes to see her. She was with a tall man who stroked a harp like a tai chi instructor waving tranquility out from thin air. The girl herself sat on the ground, flapping exotic fans as she sang to a small crowd of children.

"As I said, her voice reminded me of a scream. I know I heard one just before I died. I'm sure of it. I remember being with someone I love, but it's not Wade. So tell me, Guy. Who was I with the night I died?"

Chapter Six

I DID SOMETHING I wasn't supposed to do. I visited Wade without my angel guide. Somehow he looked older. About three years older.

A young dark-haired man was let into our home by my gentle widower. He couldn't have been more than twenty-five, but his rebellious jacket and torn jeans looked like he was about to cruise some back room.

"You said your name was James?" Wade asked.

"That's close enough," the young man replied.

"And the cost is two hundred dollars?"

"Yes, paid up front."

My husband had hired a rent boy. What a strange thing to do. So out of character for the man I'd spent eighteen years with. I'm dead for a moment and he's calling up the candy shop! He led this plaything to our bedroom.

"I've never done this sort of thing before," my old man admitted.

"Neither have I."

"Seriously?"

"No, I mean I do this all the time. For money, I mean. Not that I don't do it for no money. But while I'm at work, I do it for money."

"James, you're a newbie."

"Well, it's not like I haven't had sex before."

"Yeah, but I could've picked someone from an internet singles site if I wanted just anyone. Today I was going to treat myself."

"Please don't send me back to the agency. I'm really good at it."

"At what in particular?"

"At anything you want, big boy."

Wade screeched with laughter. So did I. Fortunately no one here could hear me.

"Sir!" James shouted. "I'm ready and willing. At your service one hundred percent."

Wade laughed louder.

"Mr. James, you're selling yourself too hard."

"I always believe that I should give my all."

"Looking at you, sweetheart, half of what you've got on offer is enough for my two hundred dollars."

"What is it you'd actually like me to do for you, Peter?"

Peter? My Wade had a fake name for this occasion? If he had to have a pseudonym, surely he could have come up with something better than Peter. Trojan, perhaps? Conrad or Miles. But Peter?

"James, I think I need a spit and polish."

Oh please! He might have given himself a lame name, but his dialogue was straight out of forgotten VHS porn. Long live Jeff Stryker.

James undid Wade's belt before leisurely unbuttoning his fly. I should have picked my visiting hours more carefully. Maybe when Wade was brushing his teeth or at work. I would have preferred a killer hangover to watching the man of my life "getting it on" with someone earning money to pay his university fees.

"Yes." James drooled. He lingered on the middle vowel for added effect.

No. I watched him slobber over his lips. I left the vulgar scene and made my way to the lounge room.

A bit shabby. New furniture was scattered here and there, but none of it matched our old lounge suite. My favorite framed movie poster, which usually hung above the armchair, was replaced by some abstract monstrosity.

There was, however, a few *Modern Living* periodicals in a pile on the characterless coffee table. Featured on the cover of the magazine sitting on top was a kitchen to die for, if that was at all possible in my current circumstance. Dark red cupboard doors with knotted wood benchtops. Divine! I crouched to take a closer look, only to notice the mysterious date. This edition was published a year and a half after I'd died!

From the bedroom, Wade sounded like a soprano aiming for a note he couldn't reach. I snuck back to have a look. I knew every expression on his face. Bliss. Delight. Ecstasy. He was moving on with his life without me.

"Wade, I know you can't hear me, but maybe in your mind, you can. I still love you very much. And I miss you." They kept bonking. "I'm with Guy, and even Mannix is here, but... What's James doing? Really? Wade, I never knew that was a kink you were into. You should have said something.

Anyway, I'll ignore the riding crop and the leather horse head. No, don't neigh as well. It's not the way I want to remember you."

"Ouch!" my husband shouted.

"Sorry," said James.

"This was a silly idea."

"I can leave if you want."

"No. Stay. I meant the equine paraphernalia was a silly idea."

"What made you want to use it?"

"I borrowed it from a friend. He's into all that weird shit. He said I'd like it."

The rent boy helped my husband take off the ridiculous mask. But soon he was in rhythm again, taking my old man for a spin.

"If I could take back anything, it would be you," I mumbled. "My week without you has been hard. But here you are more than a year later without *me*, coming to terms with things a bit too effortlessly for my liking!"

I took a deep breath and turned my back on the sordid scene.

"I miss you. I miss you with me, and how you made me feel. I miss making you the most important human being on the planet. James, stop moaning, I'm trying to have a private moment here. Wade, most of all, I miss the synergy we had together. It's hard without you. So much harder without you in the Afterlife. Or me here at home with you. I'd give anything to be mortal again."

I turned to the bedroom door, still not facing their lovemaking.

"What I really want to say, Wade, is that I'm still madly and deeply in love with you. I hope you still love me too."

"Do you really expect Wade to hear you?"

Joshua stood in angel form in front of me.

Chapter Seven

"WHAT ARE YOU doing here?" I asked.

"The question is, Adam, what are you doing here?"

"Visiting my husband."

"That's not what I mean, lover boy. How did you get here without Guy holding your hand?"

"I don't know. I just wanted to be here, and here I was."

Joshua stared like a parent whose child was lying. "Peculiar, I must say."

Wade and James's moans were getting louder.

"Your man knows how to get into position and accept his rewards."

"Thanks, Joshua. That's why I'm not facing them. I've seen enough."

"It's a shame. There's a lot to learn here."

The demon started making his way toward the bed, but I reached out to stop him.

"What are you doing here?" I asked.

"Finding love in all the wrong places."

"Very funny. This is *my* home. What are you doing here?"

"Well, my flustered mortal, I came looking for you."

"For me?"

"Yes, for you! I have a use for you." He peered at the lovers. "Wade is quite gifted, isn't he? Where did he learn that move from?"

"Josh!"

"What is it, little Adam?"

"You're overstaying your welcome."

"By the looks of the shenanigans in front of me, you are too."

He snapped his fingers. In an instant, we were at the Carousel. I was tipsy, and by the look of Joshua's droopy wing, so was he. A blonde-haired woman with bosoms large enough to keep her from drowning served us two glasses of beer.

"But I don't drink beer," I slurred.

"It's ginger beer, Adam. Alcoholic ginger beer."

I drank. Its tangy fizz tickled my tongue.

"Will that be all, gentlemen?" our barmaid asked.

"Another round, my dear," the demon replied. "Knowing my friend's mouth, he'll sip this cleaner than a—"

"Joshua!"

"Only kidding. But we will need another round."

The woman curtsied. I noticed she wore plats. Her buxom body made its way back to the bar.

A young man sat on the floor, bouncing his hands frenetically on a set of bongos. His fingernails were chipped and dirty. His hair could've oiled a Swiss timepiece. His eyes were as wide as Frisbees. He was the lad that charity overlooked.

There were no other patrons in the bar. On our table sat a toy rocking horse in an edible shade of candy pink. I touched its base, and somehow, I felt it was longing to gallop away rather than repeat its swaying action back and forth. It peered at me with its beady eyes as the rhythmic beatnik started reciting.

Our lives are stuck behind a veil.
Our lives are stuck behind a veil.
Our lives are a canvas without any paint.
Our lives are a canvas without any paint.
We are slaves until we find the door,
Going around and around and around.

The wayward bongo player stopped beating his drum. But like the toy horse, he began to sway with the precision of a metronome.

"Why is life a nightmare whenever I'm with you, Joshua?"

"Bitter and twisted, that's me!"

Beware your friends.
Beware your friends.

"Oh brother!" I said to myself.

Because your friend may know the truth.

We stared at the makeshift musician. He watched us as he kept his body still. Two more glasses of ginger beer were plonked on our table, even though we'd hardly touched the others.

"Do you think he'll start again?" I asked the barmaid.

"Never can tell," she replied. "Sometimes he just sits and does nothing, then leaves. Other times he sits quietly until poetry possesses him." She left us.

"Now, Josh, why were you trying to find me?"

"We need to talk."

I smugly leaned back.

"Adam, you mean a lot to Guy."

"I know. He means a lot to me as well. He's my guardian after all."

"And he means a lot to me too."

"Really, Josh? You called him an alcoholic do-gooder."

"Well..."

"And you're not helping him by going on and on about his missing parents. And you're not helping him by avoiding your husbandly bedroom duties. Frankly, as a boyfriend, you're not coming up with the goods."

"I give him a lot of love, Adam."

"Really? The sort of trumped-up love that promises but never delivers!"

"Oh you're one to talk."

"Yes, I am. I had a successful marriage for nearly nineteen years. And we'd still be together making love if I didn't die."

"My lips are sealed."

"And what's that supposed to mean?"

I wanted to travel, but my dream is gone, gone.
I wanted to write, but my dream is gone, gone.
I wanted a lover, but she too is gone, gone.
I wanted a lover, but she too is gone.

"Is there an antidote to that man?" the demon joked.

"Shoving his bongos down his throat," I replied. "Now, you suggested I didn't have a successful relationship."

He finished his first glass in one gulp. "I spoke out of turn, Adam."

"Did I hear that right, Josh? Did it sound vaguely like an apology? Yes, you did speak out of turn. So you admit I had a better relationship than you and Guy."

"Only because Guy is too good for me."

The secret of the veil keeps us from seeing.
But in its place, we keep on believing.

"Shut up!" we yelled in unison.

Bongo man stared blankly at us.

"Joshua, why did you say you're not good enough for Guy?"

"Look at me, Adam. Guy is the kindhearted angel who goes out of his way to guide lost souls. And who am I? Nothing more than a demon. I disguise myself as something better to 'keep up with the Joneses' if you like. But who am I kidding?" He looked to the poet who gently tapped a background beat momentarily, before pointing to himself. "So this washed-up loser plays games. This washed-up loser keeps him on his toes. I avoid reuniting him with his parents so he has a reason to stay with me."

"Where are they?"

"In the Underworld." The toy horse rocked of its own accord. "But don't tell him, Adam. It would break his heart if he knew where they were."

"The Underworld? What the hell is the Underworld? Is there an eternal fire? Should I bring something to barbecue?"

"The Underworld is not what you think it is."

"So why did you tell me where Guy's parents are?"

"Because I need someone to help me get them out of there. And I know you'd do anything for him. Besides, I don't want my darling involved. He's an angel. It's too risky."

"More risky than being in love with a demon?"

"I'm changing. Adam, don't look at me like that. I mean it. Adam! No, seriously. Okay, I'm trying to change, but being blunt comes easy. It's the only way I know people will listen to me."

I reached for his hand. "Take it, Josh. Please."

He did.

"I'm taking a stab in the dark here. Is 'blunt' how others talked to you when you were younger?"

"Let's not talk about my childhood, if you don't mind."

I nodded.

He let go of my hand as we sipped our beers.

"I guess you are in love with Guy. You're going out of your way to rescue his parents. Still, he deserves better treatment."

"You can talk!"

"What do you mean?"

"Adam, you were a slut!"

His hand snapped over his mouth and covered it faster than a mousetrap.

"No, I wasn't. I was a loving caring partner!"

The demon shook his head. "Oh please, your underwear went up and down more times than a Broadway curtain."

My mouth fell open.

He slapped my face. "Delusions, be gone!"

Chapter Eight

"Guy, was I playing around in my final days?"

"What do you remember?"

"Hardly anything. Joshua said..."

"Joshua?"

It was morning teatime, and Guy had me over for cake and coffee. As we sat, he began leaning in his chair, and there was the faint smell of marijuana in his apartment.

"Yeah, Joshua said something about me being a slut when he came and saw me."

"What? Downstairs in your apartment? That coward never came up to see me."

"It wasn't in my apartment."

"Well, where then?"

"Um. I went to visit Wade."

An iced bun slipped out of his hand while the rest of him stayed perfectly still, as if he was posing for an artist. I jumped up, headed for his kitchen, and grabbed a tea towel.

"Guy, talk to me." I cleaned up around him. "Hello. Anyone home in there? Guy, are you all right?"

He sat up straight. "How did you see Wade without my divine help?"

"I don't know. I wanted to see him, and before I knew it, I was in my apartment back in Sydney, watching him entertain men half his age."

"I need a joint."

"Haven't you had one already?"

"Adam, my boyfriend has abandoned me, but for some reason, he's seeing you. I'm so close to meeting my parents, yet so far. And on top of that, the soul I'm supposed to be looking after is developing his own powers. I need a joint!"

"There's Irish liqueur in your kitchen. How about a nip in our coffees? Forget the joint."

He nodded.

I added a fair drop to our mugs and sat back down again.

"Now let's start at the beginning, Adam. Why is my rat of a boyfriend seeing you?"

"I promised I wouldn't tell."

"Then I need a joint."

"Okay. He wanted to talk to me about your reunion with your parents."

Guy took a large gulp of his alcoholic coffee.

"I don't think Josh is as bad as I first thought," I said.

"Oh come on, Adam. You're like two siblings baiting each other."

"Yeah, but we're actually talking now. And I've realized that he does love you in his own twisted way."

Guy put down his mug. We sat for what seemed forever until he gave a serene smile. I hugged him.

"I trust your judgment. Please be right on this."

I held him tighter. His cheek nestled on mine as he softly hummed. His wings embraced me. I closed my eyes. His talcum powder scent put me in some childhood safe place. A place where Wade's younger men escapades didn't matter.

"Guy."

"Yes, Adam."

"Was I cheating on Wade during my last days?"

"Let me ask you something, my friend."

"Oh. Not now! Can't you just answer like a normal person?"

He moved his face away from mine, yet he still held me. With red eyes, he peered through me as if I were glass.

"Are you a good ancestor, Adam?"

"Huh?"

"Are you a good ancestor?"

"That sounds like the weed talking."

"Trust me, I'm more coherent than you realize."

"Then why are you asking me if I'm a good ancestor?"

"Adam, you're an only child. But you have cousins. What will their kids remember you for?"

"For being a loving husband to Wade, and being very happy in life."

"Go on."

"Ah, let's see now. For taking up acting as a hobby. For being kind and generous. For having a wicked sense of humor. For having a happy home. For lots of things really."

"Mostly positive things?"

"Yeah. I guess."

"Make sure you do everything in your power to stop those positive footsteps from fading."

"But, Guy, did I cheat on Wade?"

"And there lies the dilemma. Do your family and friends remember you as a happy husband, or a disloyal spouse?"

"So I did cheat?"

"I didn't say that."

"Yes, you did."

"Did I?" His face contorted.

"Guy, you just asked me if my friends and family will remember me as a happy husband or a disloyal spouse."

"I guess I did." His head tilted momentarily. "Regardless, Adam, how will you be remembered?"

"For goodness sake, how should I know? It never occurred to me to visit them."

"Then think this through carefully. What have you left unfinished in the mortal world?"

"Wait a second." I stood, taking a gleaming custard tart from the plate. I took a bite, chomped, and then swallowed. "A moment ago, you were freaking out because through some magical disposition I've worked out how to visit Earth. Now you're telling me to go back down there and leave the mark of a saint."

"Adam, one of your main religions states…"

"Oh here we go. Can't you just answer a question straight up?"

"Like I was saying, one of Earth's main religions states that if you do something against God, God will forgive you. But if you do something against another person, God won't forgive you until that other person forgives you."

"God? What god? I've been here over a week and I haven't seen him. Or her."

"You've missed the point."

"I have to be good to everyone and leave no baggage on the carousel. Blah, blah, blah. I get it, Guy."

"Promise me we'll go together next time you visit Wade. I'm your guardian angel. I'll help you find answers..." He stopped again, as if someone had pressed his pause button.

"Why do you keep doing this? Ground control to Guy. Do you read me? Over."

"Of course!"

"For the love of Cher, what is it?"

"That has to be it."

"That has to be what?"

"I know why you don't need me to help you spy on the mortal world!"

Chapter Nine

"YOU DON'T REALIZE how much I appreciate this, Adam," Mannix said. "Guy's become a lost cause. He hasn't shown up for days."

I was surrounded by hordes of lost souls on those conveyor belts. There were too many moving toward me. I regretted promising that I'd help out at the Guest Welcome Center, feeling as trapped as a zoo animal.

Bewildered looks turned into excited chatter. This mismatched array of individuals resembled various extras waiting to be told which studio they were to report to.

A tribal man held a spear with the same hand that sported a watch. He came to the front of the line. As he peered at the time, I realized he had one of those communication devices popular when I was alive.

"Do you have reception here?" he asked.

"Not for mobile devices," I replied. Mannix nodded in agreement. "But there'll be old-fashioned telephones at your lodgings."

"So where are my gods in this version of Heaven?"

"You know, I've asked that myself many times."

He tapped his watch, but when the screen didn't light up, he took it off and handed it to me. I gave it to Mannix, who in return, passed me a clipboard and folder.

"I was building a hut with my sons when a storm hit." He appeared solemn.

"It's okay, Spatch I believe your name is."

He nodded.

"All will come to light in good time. For the moment, can you please step behind me and join the group of other tribal clans and flapper girls? Your team leader will take you to your new homes."

"Why the flapper girls?"

"The Tribal Quarter and the Art Deco Sector are right next to each other."

"What a strange layout you have in Heaven." He strode past me.

"You're doing well, Adam," said Mannix. He patted me on the shoulder.

"One down and about a hundred more to go," I noted. "Why are so many people dying?"

My young friend shrugged.

"Hmm, another mystery."

He gestured the next in line to come forward.

"Mannix, can I ask you something else?"

"Can it wait?"

"It can, but just let me ask you the question and we can talk about it later."

"What is it?"

"Did you know I was a slut just before I died?"

Several of the souls near the front of the line listened for the reply.

"Are you confessing or asking?"

"Asking."

"No, Adam, I didn't know that. Did sleeping with me spark your inner tramp?"

More of the newly dead stopped talking to listen.

"Apparently. I just don't remember what happened."

Mannix turned his back on the newly deceased, gesturing me to do the same. "Adam, did you find it strange that Guy didn't welcome you personally when you got here?" He kept his tone low.

"It never crossed my mind."

"I don't think he's been watching you for a while. He said something about you trying to find nirvana, but that was ages ago. Since then he hasn't talked about you, and trust me, he talks about you a lot."

"But he seems to think I was a slut. Maybe that's why he stopped talking about me."

"Maybe. But he also didn't know you were dead. He thinks the world of you, Adam. Guy should have known you'd be here. It's not like him to let you arrive on the conveyor belts."

"Why are you stressing about being a slut?" yelled a teenager in knee-high boots. "At least you had fun before you died. My parents kept grounding me."

"But I had a husband."

"Did he know?"

"I don't know, although…"

"You old folk are so square. And you're gay! Sleeping around is your sport."

I wanted to slap that girl into next week.

"Adam, maybe you and Wade experimented after me," Mannix replied.

"I don't think that's what Josh meant when he told me."

"Joshua told you! What did he say?"

"He avoided the issue shortly after he brought it up."

"Where's your husband now?" asked a stunning woman. She wore a black cocktail dress and was standing behind the vampy teen.

"He's still alive."

"What a shame you can't put your fears to rest by asking him."

"At least you're free," said the girl. "You can go out and get laid every night, if nights happen here."

I nodded.

"There you go. I think that tribal warrior had eyes for you. I'm sure you can fill up your dance card."

Mannix chuckled.

"But his heart is yearning," said the woman.

"I think he should explore older sex," proclaimed a drunk elderly lady next to the pleasant woman. She held a champagne glass in her hand. "I mean, look at him. He's no spring chicken, but he's not too old to be single again."

"He looks as old as my parents," the shameless teen replied.

"I think he's handsome," said the elegant woman.

"Oh, he's all right," replied the timeworn drunk. She looked around, then yelled to a droopy-chested man wearing tennis shorts and nothing else. "You'd do him, wouldn't you, love?"

He gave me two thumbs-up.

I wanted to vomit.

The teen addressed me. "He's so old his legs would crack as you tried to lift them above…"

"Yes, I get the picture," I interrupted.

"I'd do him," called another man from one of the other conveyor belts.

He stood like an adventure hero from a timeless movie, with a pistol in one hand and short-cropped blond hair that demanded soulful caressing.

This gentle male was about thirty. His loose white shirt was slightly ripped, while the denim that clutched his lower half left nothing to the imagination.

"He's much better than grandpa with the ugly shorts," said the teen.

"If you don't take up his offer, I will," slobbered the alcoholic.

I looked to Mannix who seemed to be in shock, then turned toward my new male god.

"Thank you," I shouted.

"Not you," he shouted back. "I meant Mannix."

"It's David," Mannix whispered.

"Who's David?" I asked.

"Someone from my past, Adam."

"Someone who still has your heart captured by the look of things."

My friend half smiled. "I'm going to his conveyor belt. Will you be all right by yourself?"

"Mannix, go and do what you need to do. I'll be fine."

He ambled over like a lost puppy and carefully processed the waiting souls. David stood patiently in line.

"So you and him had something once?" asked the vampy teen. She stepped forward.

"My husband and I were infatuated with Mannix a while ago."

"That grin says it all!" She gave me a high five.

"What is this?" screamed a manic voice. "A homosexual haven?"

"What a dreadful screech," the drunk woman stated. "With a voice like that, she could join a death-metal band."

"What kind of Heaven is this? No God. No pearly white gates." This American accent was getting closer. "Who's in charge here?"

The people in front were doing their best to not be knocked aside as a short woman in a white shirt pushed her way to the front.

"Who the hell are you?" asked Teen Girl.

"And who are you to ask, you slut of Satan?"

I jumped in before my vampy friend's fist hit this unsavory woman. But I copped her punch in the side of my neck.

"Oh, I'm sorry."

"And they call *me* a queer basher."

"Let me guess," I said, sounding as if I was being choked. "You're from sometime in the twentieth century, right?"

"Of course. Who isn't?"

"Well, I'm not."

"What is this circus?" She turned to the teenager. "And what kind of parents let you out in that gear?"

"Really?" the teen replied. "Did you look in a mirror before you walked out the door?"

"She's got a point," I added. "It looks like your hair hasn't been washed in years."

"Well, trust a sinner like you to worry about what my hair looks like. I'm sure you have plenty of hairdresser friends. And why are you here in God's land?"

"It looks like you've got your work cut out for you," said the drunk. She tried to sip her champagne, but half of it dripped down her jacket.

"Alcohol is the devil's brew."

"Then why did Jesus turn water into wine?" the lady in the cocktail dress queried.

"Jesus does what Jesus does."

"Wow, such a well thought-out argument," I said.

"It looks like I'm the only one worthy of being here. Where is the Lord? We'll get this place back on track. There'll be no room for queers like you."

"Who are you, you whack job?" I studied the paperwork on my clipboard. "I can't see a foul-mouthed religious nutter on my list."

"My name is Mary. Like the mother of our savior. I changed it legally."

"Why didn't you just call yourself Jesus? With your inflated sense of self, why pick a mere mortal to name yourself after?"

"Just because you don't know whether you're Arthur or Martha, doesn't mean we're all gender confused." She looked to the small crowds gathered behind me. "I'm not joining the team of jungle men over there. Who knows what *they* worship."

"I don't think I should leave you with anyone here." I found her details and read. She hadn't been assigned to any sector of the Afterlife. Mannix was busy talking to David so I didn't call for his help.

"I don't care where I go, as long as I can preach the word."

"God botherer, extraordinaire," groaned the teen.

"Listen, young lady, our Lord can save anyone's soul!"

"Well, when he gets around to saving yours, let me know," I declared. "Turning you into a decent human being will the biggest miracle I've ever seen, and trust me, I've seen a few!"

Chapter Ten

"SO WHO IS greeting the new arrivals today, Mannix?" Guy asked.

"A couple of the team leaders. Elliot has been at me for a while to take charge, so he's working with Jesse."

"Is Elliot ready?"

"Under Jesse's command, he'll be fine."

"Are you ready?" I asked.

Mannix stayed silent. At any moment, we would be joined by David, the mysterious man from yesterday's arrivals. Our young friend wanted support for this meeting, so Guy and I sat on blankets ready for a friendly picnic.

"It strikes me odd that you're not confident enough to meet David on your own," I said. "When Wade and I first met you, you had sexual swagger."

"There was someone who—" he began.

"Wait a second." Guy had interrupted. "I need to pour wine. Deep and meaningful conversations always require wine."

Mannix and I shared concerned glances as the angel plunged a corkscrew into a bottle of red. He poured liberally before handing us our glasses.

"As I was saying, someone told me I wasn't attractive enough."

"What!" I cried. "Was this person blind?"

"How old were you at the time?" Guy asked.

"Nineteen."

"That's an impressionable age. Too young to be told something like that."

"My gorgeous friend," I began, "Wade and I met you when you were thirty-one. To us, you were a sex god!"

"Adam, sleeping with you both was a big step for me. You know that."

"And what about David?"

"We never slept together."

"So like Wade and I, David was just another of many, I suspect, waiting to help you reach your potential."

Mannix smiled coyly. "What about you, Guy?"

"What about me what?" he asked.

"How are you and Joshua?"

"That's what I call taking the heat off yourself," I noted. "Actually, that's a good question. You and Josh. What's the story?"

"I'm starting to feel like this whole love thing is a sham," Guy replied. "Don't look at me like that, Mannix. Obviously for you it isn't. But for me, it's a strange game with peculiar results."

"I wouldn't put Joshua in the dustbin yet. He's working in your best interests."

"He is," Mannix concurred. "Trust us."

"Joshua is that charismatic guy I longed for but couldn't have. And then I had but wasn't sure exactly why I wanted him."

"So what is it about him you love?" I asked.

"I bitch about his wicked sense of humor, but inside he makes me laugh. Whether he's himself or in his angel disguise, he's still a man who people look twice at. And he's mine, all mine! But is that enough?"

No one answered. Soft gray clouds gave our park a lonely feel. There were a few others enjoying chicken and champagne in the distance, while a man in a singlet strummed his guitar as they ate. His sentimental tune rode the light breeze in our direction, creating the perfect mood for our open discussion.

"Guy, I need to know something," I said. Mannix eyed me as if he knew what I was going to ask. "Were you watching over me when I died?"

The angel nearly spat out his wine, then casually remarked, "Of course."

"So you saw my death and what led to it?"

"Why are you so curious?"

"I thought I was asking the questions, Guy."

"Sorry," said Mannix. "I brought the subject up with Adam. I just thought—"

"I am *his* guardian angel. I stayed by his side."

We left the topic alone. The people in the distance laughed. Trees rustled. And the guitar strumming continued. Then after a silence, I changed the subject.

"I haven't been in a green field with you, Guy, since I was a kid."

"And you were a child that needed lots of guidance," he replied. His mood, normal.

"That's right, I heard about this," said Mannix. "You used to visit Adam when he was alive."

"He was *my* guardian angel."

Guy grinned as he topped up his wine. Mannix and I were only halfway through our first glass.

"Remember what you used to call me when you were a child?" he asked.

"Mr. Guy," I replied.

"Were you being respectful to your elders, Adam?" Mannix asked.

"I'm not sure." I grinned back at my guardian. "Back then I didn't know about angels. I thought he was a fairy. You know, like a tooth fairy or something."

"And I used to tell him if he wanted to think of me as a fairy, then I was a fairy."

"Not much has changed," Mannix joked.

"You're one to talk!" I replied. "You know, Guy, you were like a big brother to me. A much older big brother."

"I know, Adam. As a child you needed me, and I enjoyed playing parent."

"And I needed you as an adult, and without hesitation, you were there."

We clinked glasses.

"Oh no," said Mannix.

"What?" I asked.

But I didn't need the answer. That dreamy blond man I saw yesterday was making his way toward us with a bottle of wine in hand.

"Oh good," said Guy. "I was worried we'd run out of alcohol."

I opened a plastic container of mouthwatering cheeses I had cut into bite-size pieces, just because I was bored that morning, and offered the first piece to David. He picked some blue vein, eyed it like a chef scrutinizing an essential ingredient, then popped it in his mouth. His groans of culinary pleasure sounded sexual. I handed the container to Guy without taking my eyes off the young man.

Mannix was about to stand, but lover boy eased himself next to him on the blanket. Guy was already pouring both our guest and himself a glass of red. Mannix introduced us before tasting a slice of camembert.

"Were you in the armed forces?" I asked David.

"What do you mean?" he queried.

"You're Australian, like Mannix and I, yet when you arrived yesterday you had a pistol in your hand. What's an Australian citizen doing with a pistol?"

"I don't know, Adam. I'm as confused about why I held a gun as you are."

"Yeah, it's a bummer that. I'm still trying to put together the last days of my demise." I sympathized.

"David, have you thought of any reasons why you had a pistol in your hand?" Guy asked.

"And why your shirt was ripped?" Mannix added.

"It's all a blur except for the really weird part. I was being fired at by a plane in a field."

"You weren't a soldier when I knew you."

"And I'm sure I wasn't a soldier any time in my life."

"What else do you remember?" Guy asked.

"Running as fast as I could while trying to fire back with that pistol." He took another piece of blue vein. "Now why would a plane be firing at an administrative assistant?"

"A gun and a ripped shirt," I repeated. "And a plane firing at you. That's more confusing than my last memories. Are you sure you don't know why?"

"Beats me," he shrugged.

"Well, I'm glad you're here, with us," Mannix said. He took the cheese from David's hand and placed it in his love interest's mouth.

"Why didn't you two have sex?" Guy slurred, inebriated.

David laughed while Mannix gave Guy a quick death stare.

"What I'd like to know is how you two met," I asked.

"He was the nude model in my art class," David replied.

"I was a student in that art class as well. How come I never met you?"

"I met David about a year before I met you, Adam."

"Do you always pick up trade when you model?" Guy garbled.

Now David looked as if he'd seen a ghost, so I popped another piece of cheese in his hand while giving my guardian a stern look.

"I'm sorry, David," Guy said. "But I think I'm going to be a nude model. It's the best way to—"

"What Guy means, David, is—" Mannix looked into space to find the rest of his sentence. "—is that I meet a lot of people through my modeling."

"Yes, he does. And for some reason, they're always infatuated with him."

"I don't know if I was infatuated with him," David said. "Charmed by him, but I wasn't obsessed."

"Really? Adam and his husband were totally—"

"More wine, Guy?" I didn't wait for an answer. I refilled his glass with the bottle David brought.

"Thanks." He brought the glass to his wine-stained lips. "Now, David, did you and Mannix—?"

"We already answered that, Guy," Mannix replied.

"Date! Did you and David date? That's all I was going to say."

"We went on a couple of dates," replied our guest. "The first one was in a restaurant. Egyptian food, I think. Mannix wandered in wearing burgundy and black, and I couldn't take my eyes off him. We chatted and drank, but somehow we didn't get drunk." He briefly smirked at Guy. "Mannix, you found your old toy train set at your parents' place that day, and I was encouraging you to set it up for our next date."

"You *remember* that?" Our bashful friend was chuffed.

"And you never dug out the train set for our next date."

"We're adults, David. I thought you were joking. It's not a thing for grown men to do on a date."

"You're never too old to play," I said.

"Adam's right." He tasted his wine while gazing at Mannix. My friend gazed back as if he'd found his safe place. And in the distance, the guitar still sang to us.

In their look I saw the countless times Wade and I shared glances. When the world was void of sense, I had a pair of caring eyes to look into, telepathically telling me everything was okay. They were eyes that never judged, that comforted me. Oh how I missed my husband.

"Toy trains," Guy said. "Is that a metaphor for something?"

I tried to take his wineglass away from him, but he clutched it as if it was as precious as long-lost treasure.

"On second thought, hold on to that glass," I said. "You're going to need it."

"What do you mean, Adam?" He peered over his shoulder. "Who's that woman?"

Striding toward us with purpose was Mary.

"Oh no, not her!" Mannix groaned. "I was keeping my distance from her yesterday."

"I know. I had to deal with her myself as you two lovebirds caught up on personal history."

"Why is she coming to us, Adam?"

"To preach fire and brimstone," said David.

"No, it's Guy's wings," I replied. "She's found an angel."

"It's about time I found someone holy!" she called from a distance. Her shrill voice was louder than a megaphone.

I stood and held out the cheese container. She brushed it aside and sat next to Guy.

"Adam, who is this woman?" he asked. His shock resembled that of a child being told he's about to be sent to boarding school.

"Mary's my name." She shook Guy's reluctant hand. "These men are homosexual. Why are they allowed to corrupt the Lord's own country?"

"A judgmental Christian. Gosh, I haven't seen one of those here for a while."

"I've never met one," I said.

"I read about them," David admitted. "Somehow last century there were people who claimed to be Christian, yet they disapproved of our kind."

"What are you talking about?" Mary cried, deafening us in the process. "Jesus would never approve of any of you. God made Adam and Eve, not—"

"—Adam and Steve," said Guy.

"That's a new one," Mannix stated. "It rhymes, but it will never catch on."

"They were known as fundamentalists, but they weren't always Christian," said David. "For some reason, they kept finding new people to hate."

"You misguided fools," she yelled. "You are hating God by your wicked acts!"

"Would you like a glass of wine, Mary?" I asked. "No, really, you need one."

"I suppose you had your own depraved queer religion."

"My husband and I were interfaith."

"Your husband? What kind of backward country did you come from?"

"She's for real, isn't she?" Mannix asked. He stood and studied her like a museum piece. David soon joined him.

"Imagine if she came from our time," I said. "She'd be locked up for lunacy. Spitting words of hate in some psychiatric ward. Even in her home country."

"I am not a loony!" she yelled.

"Mary, have you listened to yourself?" said Guy quietly. He sounded surprisingly sober. "You are the fish out of water here. No intelligent being would ever come to the conclusions you're coming to."

She was listening.

"You must have lived a sheltered life where you never asked questions. You just accepted what was told to you by similar fools."

Mannix poured her a glass of wine, while I offered her cheese. She gobbled down some goat's feta.

"And many decades after you died, people like you were no longer around. People accepted what the Great Spirit created and were happy in just living. They didn't complicate things. And most of all, they didn't hate."

"No one can truly hate something they didn't once love." David was being philosophical.

"Mannix, I like this man," I declared. "Keep this one."

Mary tried a piece of brie. "I see the light," she said calmly. "You may have wings, but you too have been blinded by evil. You are one of them. You are just as queer as your friends are, with their queer collection of cheese."

"What's wrong with our cheese?" I asked.

"These flavors soften you. You are not eating men's cheese!"

"No one say anything, as much as you'd like to."

Mannix and David joined me in a juvenile snigger.

"And I'll be your savior, you misguided angel. It is God's will. My mission is to save your homosexual soul! That will sort this place out."

"How?" Guy asked. His wings fluttered.

"Once I cast the devil out of you, his hold on these queer boys will be gone!"

He held up his half-empty glass. I filled it promptly.

Chapter Eleven

I DID IT again. My ghostly self went to visit Wade. And even though I promised Guy that I would never go back to Earth without him, I really didn't want his drunken musings playing with my mind while I saw my husband.

I checked the date on a magazine on the coffee table. Fortunately, it was only two months after my last visit. I couldn't bear the thought of him growing old too quickly without me.

The publication was one of those gay journals aimed at twenty-somethings featuring skimpy fashion spreads and an article on a prima donna. Very unusual for our household. He might have been only two months older, but my Wade seemed to be wishing he were twenty years younger.

A few empty takeaway boxes sat with dirty dishes in the kitchen sink. The carpet needed a clean as there was a dark stain I didn't want to ponder on. And he'd moved some of the ornaments in the display cabinet. *What happened to my angel figurines?*

The tart smell of cigarette smoke hit me. Nosing around the lounge room was a bright young thing who was barely old enough to work out his sexuality. I freaked out when he flicked ash in a crystal vase. He sat and reached into the elastic band that passed for his shorts and pulled out his phone.

"Ricky, I'm bored. Wade just passed out again. He hasn't got the stamina. No, not like when I first met him. Okay, okay, it was only a week ago. But even then he had the stamina that you have, Ricky. Yeah, I want you to come over. I can't ask him. He's asleep. Of course he won't mind. Yeah, there's some porn here. Not a lot. We'll think of something. Okay, see ya soon. Oh yeah, and bring those pills you got for us. Okay, bye."

This fetus grabbed the remote control and turned on the television. He channel-surfed insistently before stopping at one of those lame talk shows that confuse infomercials with content.

I wandered into the bedroom and saw Wade naked, slumped facedown on the floor. The bed was unmade, and the sheets smelled like they hadn't been washed for weeks. The duvet cover didn't match the pillow slips and two of the framed pictures on the wall were noticeably crooked.

The phone in the lounge room rang and quickly switched to a retro answering machine we never owned. I peered from the bedroom and watched spring chicken take no interest in the phone. He was still flicking ash.

"Wade, it's Maude. This is my seventh call in a week, and I still haven't spoken to you. Yes, that's right, I don't take text messages as communication. Especially when you write 'I'm fine, Maude.' I don't believe you're fine. Adam's been gone for two years, and I know it's hard, but you can't go on like this. You just can't.

"Now, the next time I come over, I want you to answer the door. I knew you were home last time because I heard the TV when I entered your building. I'll bring our favorite. A bottle of gin. You need a good talk and a good cry. End of story. In fact, I'll come over tomorrow night. Okay, that's all I have to say. Hope you're all right. Bye for now."

Ricky arrived to entertain the thing in our lounge room. Okay, to be honest, I did watch them for a while. Free sex show in my old apartment. I'd have given them a seven for stamina but only a four for technique.

I strolled back to the bedroom where Wade snored softly. I lay on the floor beside him.

"My beautiful man," I said. "My beautiful man, it's me, Adam. I'm okay. I'm still with Guy and Mannix in a surrealist dream on the other side."

He stirred.

"I did something wrong, I'm told. Apparently I played around. I just can't remember. I'm sorry for whatever I did."

"Adam," he mumbled.

"Can you hear me?" I waited and waited. He didn't speak. "If I could find a way for my ghostly presence to hold you again and make you know I was here, I would. But I'm still pretty new at the 'dead' thing. Still learning. Still working it out. Just remember at the end of each day, I'm in love with you. Simple as that. I'm in love."

I shut my eyes.

"You don't believe this Guy thing, do you?"

It was my own voice. My eyes flicked open. Wade was still sleeping next to me, but arguing in our bedroom was another version of us.

"Adam, I never did."

"Not even when I told you he was in my childhood dreams?"

"Yes, that I did believe, but come on! A grown man being whisked away by an angel to the Afterlife while he's still alive. What kind of fool do you take me for?"

"But it did happen! I wouldn't lie about something like that. Think about it, Wade. Why would I risk sounding like I'd lost my marbles to the man I love?"

"I don't know. So you can start acting flakier than you already are. Divorce yourself from your responsibilities because you've seen the other side and know best!"

"That doesn't even make sense."

"All I know, Adam, is that Maude and I think you haven't coped with Mannix's death."

The scene faded. I remembered that argument. I remembered the loneliness I felt at that moment. I remembered that I began doubting my own sanity. And I remembered that things were never the same between Wade and me.

Chapter Twelve

"A HAIRY HAND with nail polish offered *you* a cupcake." I repeated the words I'd just heard.

"Adam, I know it sounds far-fetched," David replied, "but it seems to be all I remember of the last day of my life."

"And that's not the best part," Mannix added.

I fidgeted with the toy robot on our table at the Carousel. It was early afternoon, and while I still had my head going round and round trying to piece together my final days, I was listening to a tale to rival my memories.

David looked left, then right, then to me as if he was sharing a family secret. He placed his hand on mine, stopping me from toying with the red metal android.

"It was a cyanide cupcake," he said.

I stared into space.

"I know, Adam," said Mannix. "It's weird, isn't it?"

I felt unusually calm. It wasn't a sane David story. It wasn't a tale Mannix would normally believe in. But love does crazy things to those it holds on to. It makes them imagine the impossible with the credibility of a bank statement.

A flute player cast a spell over half a dozen men and women swaying nearby, who looked like they'd tie-dyed stolen bedsheets from clotheslines just to wear for the occasion. Matched with the bizarre tale I was being told, this was one of those days in the Afterlife where this theater of the absurd kicked into full swing, and it still didn't faze me.

"So you were given a poison cupcake by a drag queen," I said.

"I know," David replied. "It sounds far-fetched, doesn't it?"

"But that's still not the best bit," his lover added.

"Betsy the drag queen was a double agent!"

"So who were you in this twisted tale?" I asked.

"Someone she was trying to protect when the plane came shooting at us."

He still had his hand on mine, waiting for me to respond. I peered at Mannix whose dreamy expression was aimed solely at his overly creative boyfriend.

"But it doesn't explain why someone poisoned you to protect you."

"Because he was running away from a plane that was shooting at him," Mannix replied.

He looked at me as if this made perfect sense. His vote of confidence in David warmed my heart. I too had been captivated by Wade on many storytelling occasions. His hand gestures would transmit half the tale, and his gentle tones conveyed the crucial bits. But it never mattered to me what he was saying. He could have recited a shopping list, and I still would have watched his lush lips merely exercise, before they were used during our passionate embraces later in the evening.

"Adam, you still don't get it," Mannix said.

I whizzed the propeller on top of the toy robot's head.

"Don't you see?" David continued. "Betsy had just told me she was a secret agent, and all of a sudden, the plane came from nowhere and began firing at us. She handed me a cupcake and apologized for putting me in danger. She didn't want me to be shot to death so she gave me a kinder way to die."

"How did you end up with a pistol in your hand?" I asked.

"I'm not sure."

"Can you bake poison into a cupcake?"

"Apparently," Mannix replied.

David rested his finger on his chin. "It doesn't make sense, does it?"

"But it's a great story," I said. "Keep using it and see who believes it."

"There has to be some truth in it," Mannix said.

"Yes, but you know how confused everyone is when they get here. The truth comes out in bite-size pieces and never as a full course. At least that's what I'm learning."

A man in a pin-striped suit began to dance with the bedsheet mob. They raised their arms to an unseen god and waved their hands as if voodoo had taken hold. Their new apprentice began to hum to the tune of the flute, closing his eyes to allow more of the spell to enter his core.

"It's official," I said. "This place can't get any weirder."

"And we haven't even had a drink yet," said Mannix.

"And the barmaid seems to be transfixed with the cosmic bedsheet dancers."

"I'll get us something special," said David. "I'll introduce you to my favorite summer cocktail."

He rose and made his way past the swaying hippies, stepping in rhythm with their moves. I placed the toy robot down on the table with its feet pointing forward. It sat facing Mannix as if it were about to listen to our conversation.

"He's a really cool guy," I said.

"I know." He beamed. "He has as much charisma as a whole boy band, and then some."

"So have you. Why was he so special in your previous life?"

"Because I was tongue-tied every time he came near me."

"You don't seem tongue-tied now."

He glanced at his lover. I looked too, while I moved the robot so he could see as well. As David laughed with the barman, Mannix changed the topic.

"I still don't believe Guy was keeping an eye on you when you died."

"I believe you. He didn't sound convincing the other day defending himself. But we shouldn't bring it up again. It's something he doesn't like talking about."

"Can you forgive him for not being there?"

"Mannix, I hardly remember what happened. I'm not sure there's anything to forgive. Anyway, Guy has a lot on his mind."

"Like excessive alcohol and dope?"

"Like excessive alcohol and dope."

Three reddish-pink cocktails sat in tall glasses on the bar. Just as David was about to carry them back to us, a short woman strode up to him.

"Oh dear," said Mannix.

"It's Mary the misguided Christian," I growled.

"David is keeping her at the bar."

"What a trooper!" I positioned my metal toy back to look at my friend. "Mannix, I don't understand how such a good-looking person like you had trouble talking to potential lovers your own age. I mean, you made yourself at home with Wade and I."

"Now, there's a change of topic. Adam, you were older guys. It's easier with established men. Besides, *you* were the nervous one when we met.

Remember? So I was in control of our three-way flirting, until I realized I was in over my head, so I backed away."

"How did you find your newfound confidence?"

"Age teamed up with experience, here in the Afterlife." He winked.

The flutist was joined by that annoying bongo player, as the "Age of Aquarius" mob and their pin-striped mate danced more frenetically. Their thumping feet sounded like a herd of elephants running from danger.

A geisha girl, who had been teaching a small group of people how to perform a traditional tea ceremony, glared at the dancers. She moved closer to her students and raised her voice. She was alone in her discomfort. Others in the bar seemed to enjoy the impromptu show.

Even David and Mary were clapping their hands to the bongo beat, before they carried the cocktails, alone with a glass of sparkling water, back in our direction.

"Don't fret, boys," she said, joining us at our table. "I've seen the light."

David shrugged behind Mary's back, then sat.

"So what are these delicious-looking cocktails?" I inquired.

"Strawberry-lemon mojitos, Adam. I used to make them at home for my friends on hot days."

Blueberries swam in my lush pink drink as I swirled the ice cubes with my straw. I took a sip. My taste buds were ready to sing after the first initial tang of this heavenly concoction.

"Didn't you hear what I said?" Mary was interrupting my state of bliss. "I said I've seen the light."

"Who switched it on?" I asked.

She sat next to me. "No, hear me out. I am tolerant of your lifestyle choice."

"Wow. I'm being tolerated. Not accepted, but tolerated."

"I didn't know my bisexuality was a lifestyle choice," Mannix added.

"Now, Mary, that's not what you said when we spoke at the bar," said David. "You said you learned to be accepting."

"I have," she replied. "I asked myself what would Jesus do and realized he would have walked among the sinners."

"Sorry, guys." David blushed as he spoke. "She insisted on apologizing to you both, so I brought her over."

Mary stood. "No one 'gets me' here. I'll leave you alone."

"No, Mary," I said. "Sit down."

The lovers looked at me as if I'd lost my mind.

"I want to know how your thought process got to this point."

She sat.

"Adam, I don't think I'm as curious as you are," said Mannix. He stroked my toy robot.

"I'm curious," David added. "I'm dying to know how this woman got so misguided."

"Now, Mary," I began, "you're an American religious person who lived…?"

"In the nineteen seventies," she replied.

"Wow. That's five decades before I was born."

She seemed unfazed.

"And for entertainment, you…?"

"Me and the family would go hunting."

"So you gave yourself a sense of power above other creatures."

Mannix and David giggled.

"Now hold on a second. They were just animals. They were put here for us to eat."

"A Buddhist would not agree with you."

"Don't go preaching some mumbo-jumbo religion at me. Christianity is the only true way to meet our Maker."

"Then where is he?" David asked.

"He's hiding away because he's disgusted by you sinners!"

"Now, now, Mary," I said. "No name calling."

"But that's what you are. You and that rowdy lot of misguided fools dancing around like tribal idiots next to us. You're all sinners!"

The front door of the Carousel swung open as Joshua, in his angel disguise, entered. He quickly scanned the room and saw us. Mary jumped up with a delighted squeal at this new winged creature, sounding like she'd won the jackpot in a lottery. The masquerading demon headed our way.

"It's time," he said.

"Is God here?" Mary asked.

"Joshua, meet my boyfriend, David," said Mannix. "And this here is Mary."

She shook the disguised demon's hand, then clutched onto it like it held her life savings. He tried to ease away from her grip, but she held on tighter.

"Anyway," he said. "It's time."

"Time for what?" I asked.

"Time to venture to the Underworld and meet Preston."

"The Underworld?" Mary inquired. "That sounds like a place an angel shouldn't venture to."

I handed Josh my cocktail. "Here, try this."

"I'm not thirsty."

"No, seriously. This is heaven on your tongue."

"It's my summer specialty," David added. "I make it for my friends."

Joshua reluctantly took the glass from my hand and moved it to his lips. With Mary watching, I noted his reflection in the cocktail. On cue, our deluded Christian screamed her lungs out as his angel disguise disappeared in the likeness mirrored through the drink.

She jumped around like a woman possessed. The bongo player thumped his instrument with more force, but the hippie dance troop didn't follow his beat. They stopped to see what the commotion was about.

"It's the devil!" she cried.

The other patrons seemed perplexed as the barmaid came our way.

"We don't know what came over her," I said.

Mary marched away from us, stopped, looked back, ran in a circle, and sat on the floor in the middle of bedsheet posse, shaking.

"We really need to go," Josh whispered. "Preston is waiting for us."

We stood.

"Hold on," I muttered. "I'm feeling a terrible sense of guilt about what I've just done to Mary. I've shattered her trust in angels."

"Well, get over it. We have to leave."

"I'll stay," said David.

"I'll stay too," said Mannix. He cuddled his boyfriend.

"Mannix, you need to join Adam and me," Josh dictated. "David, you seem like a man of the world, but I don't know you well. You stay here and look after the weirdo."

David nodded as Mannix reluctantly let go of him. Mary kept muttering "devil" over and over in the middle of the silent crowd. I wandered out with the others, not quite ready to meet the real entity Mary only thought she had seen.

Chapter Thirteen

"THE GATE TO Hell is a *manhole* cover!" I shrieked.

Joshua and Mannix battled with the heavy iron lid. The demon's bat wings fluttered to give him extra pull power.

In an inconspicuous laneway in the Medieval Quarter, not far from where I lived, was the entrance to evil. No fences. No warning signs. No fiery pit. Nothing as exotic as quicksand to ease your way into that place priests and nuns scare small children about. Just a manhole cover.

As the lid was carefully lifted, we could see a concrete stairway underneath. No bells or whistles. No feat of modern architecture complemented by a stylish wooden banister. No junior demons guarding the entrance. Merely pale gray concrete stairs that took us to the Underworld. We stepped down.

Its damp moldy floor needed a mop. As I stepped on its surface, I slipped and landed on my ass.

"What an inspired way to make an entrance."

The voice I heard was as smooth as Barry White's. I looked up.

"Preston, these are my friends," Joshua announced. "This is Mannix, and the one sitting down is Adam."

"Oh don't get up," his deep tone resonated. "Your mouth is at the right height to entertain me."

"And friends, this is Preston, the Leader of the Underworld."

If Rocky and Dr. Frank-N-Furter ever conceived, this was their love child. Like a high-fashion model posing on a catwalk, he stood tall, glaring at me with exquisite eyes as black as midnight. He matched his dark shade with his glossy top hat, buttoned up waistcoat, and smart trousers.

Rich gay men would sell their souls to look this good in eveningwear. His secret lay in the absence of a shirt. I longed to rub my nose through the small trail of hair that linked his chest to his navel.

And just to add glamour to his wicked grin with teeth whiter than milk, a lustrous array of charcoal-colored pearls sat elegantly around his neck. Camp had found style.

Mannix helped me to my feet.

"Joshua, can I add the young one to my collection? You can keep the other one. Too clumsy."

"Ah, but you know that's not the trade-off," the demon replied.

"Pity." He pulled out a pair of leather gloves from his trouser pocket and slipped them on. "He'd have such fun here with the other boys."

The Underworld leader stepped sideways to reveal a bright red door with a golden brass knob.

"Brace yourselves, guys," Josh said. "You're about to see the most interesting room here in the Underworld."

Preston led the way as we followed. A large iron cage full of young playful men took up most of this scarlet-painted dungeon. They gyrated in skimpy leather shorts as guitars twanged to a gravelly blues voice on a phonograph.

"As you can see, this is my harem."

"Impressive," Mannix declared.

"Like I said, you're free to join them at any time."

"No thanks."

"Are you sure?"

"Yes, really, I'm sure. Thank you. I mean, no thank you."

"Your loss." He stroked one of his specimens under the chin. "Joshua, what happened to that nice young redhead you brought down here once? He entertained our inhabitants with his vocal talents."

"Oh, he was just an acquaintance."

"Pity. I need a ginger for my collection."

"These men look so devoted," I said. "What's your secret?"

"Really, honey. Look at me. I'm drop-dead gorgeous."

I rolled my eyes.

"Only kidding, sweetheart. Let's just say, I know how to keep them happy."

"Experienced, then?"

"Of course. I came out of the closet when I was sixteen. I've been drunk ever since."

"What about stamina?"

"I have the perfect work/life balance. I divide my day into eight-hour blocks. Caffeine for eight. Alcohol for eight. Painkillers for eight." His mouth came to my ear. "It's accelerator, then brakes, then maintenance."

"Preston, we have to talk about our deal," said Joshua.

"Oh yes, that. Well, this is really not the room for meetings."

We followed single file as if our host was Mother Hen. In the next room, muzak was piped from small ceiling speakers, droning poorly realized Burt Bacharach tunes. I felt nauseous at the sound. Seated on about fifty gray cloth seats were an array of "sinners" from all walks of life, sporting individual name tags. The room itself was also painted gray.

On stage in front of them was a blonde bombshell propping up her diminished cleavage, and an attractive man with a tan suede jacket. The audience were busy taking notes while listening to a lecture about ego, its importance in day-to-day survival, its place in the Afterlife, and the best way to use it to bedazzle your enemies.

It became apparent that she was a theater director and he was a playwright.

"The Underworld has conferences?" Mannix asked.

"You sexy young entity, the Underworld *is* a conference," Preston replied. "Just wall-to-wall lectures. This evening it's 'Entertaining Strangers while Tragically Drunk.' Tomorrow morning it's 'Stealing from the Deserving,' followed by a light lunch, then 'Lust and Its Many Uses.'"

"This place really is Hell."

The presenters were now telling their eager disciples how to keep others out of the picture, no matter how brilliant their talents. In their words, "True artists are emotional train wrecks. Jump into the carriages and wreak havoc."

One slender young woman wrote this in bold letters on the cover of her notepad. As she wrote this foolish insight, she reminded me of a bitter feline—the one who doesn't rule the roost with the other alley cats but believes she should. She pursed her lips before stroking the back of her neck with painted fingernails. I even heard her purr.

"Can we leave this room?" I asked.

"Of course," Preston replied. "I have to show you the museum."

"The museum?"

"Sure. I have to keep my sinners entertained somehow between lectures."

We ambled to the next room. There were small-scale models showing empty spaces surrounded by ordinary buildings. Similar vacant lots were displayed in the photographs on the wall. And there were a few metal poles sporting signage in traffic-light colors near the middle of the floor.

"What is this?" I asked. I stared at these lifeless exhibits like a droning sleepwalker.

"It's an attraction for the guests here." Our host waved his arm around the room as if presenting the grand prize on a game show. "Welcome to our Parking Museum!"

"You've got to be kidding me."

"He's not," Joshua replied.

Mannix gazed at me with dead eyes.

"Well, that does it! The longer I stay here, the weirder the Afterlife gets. Preston, if you tell me you dress as Nana Mouskouri to do dull drag shows for those poor souls out there, it won't surprise me. Nothing can faze me here anymore."

"No, I don't do Nana," he replied. "But I do a wicked Liberace for my harem."

I felt numb.

"I never thought of dressing up for Guy," our demon said. "Is it a turn-on?"

"They love burying their faces in my mink coats. I have a full wardrobe in my office. Would you like me to show you?"

"We're really here to talk about my boyfriend's parents."

"Indulge me. Let me show you my office."

Josh shrugged. Mannix and I nodded hesitantly.

We walked through another couple of rooms until we found where all the decedent furniture had been hiding. A huge gothic desk, with carved gargoyles on its legs, overshadowed a luxurious black leather chair. On the desk were several files and a laptop. One of the folders was marked "Fetishists." Another was titled "Televangelists" while the last contained biographies of "Bank Managers."

There was one solitary painting behind his workspace. It was of himself, standing tall and looking proud in a pin-stripe business suit, but still with his black pearls on. Claret-colored flames filled the background.

"I had one of the sinners create that for me. It took him days, but I stood like a Greek statue until he was done."

"Didn't he get tired?" Mannix asked.

"You delicate young thing. Don't you know there's no rest for the wicked?"

"So where are your outfits?" Josh inquired.

Preston pushed gently against the wall with the portrait. The cement structure slid sideways to reveal a wardrobe filled with costumes that would rival any opera company. We entered.

Cowboy outfits from genuine Calamity Jane wear to plain open-assed slutty hung on the first coat hangers. A few summer frocks draped next to an Island Goddess ensemble complete with a coconut-shell bra. Military shirts were in another section, not far from an array of kinky accessories for any occasion.

"I'm impressed," said Mannix.

"I'm impressed!" I repeated.

"Good," replied our host. "This is where you will seek inspiration."

"Inspiration for what?" Mannix asked.

"Didn't Joshua tell you?"

"I thought it best that you tell them," the demon said. "After all, it was your idea."

Preston put his hands over his heart as if he was about to share his darkest secret. "I'm getting more sex than usual, so I'm feeling charitable. I need to do something nice for those poor sods."

"What?" I asked. "Are we going to be in a costume parade?"

"Oh, honey, you'll be in costume, but it's not a parade. Besides, you don't have the figure to breathe life into these garments."

"How dare you? I've been told I have a swimmer's body."

"So does salmon."

I poked out my tongue.

"So what are we doing?" Mannix queried.

"Joshua told me you both like to act, so I thought you could put on a play for the residents here."

My young friend's jaw dropped.

"What is it, dear one?" He patted Mannix on the cheek. "It will make their day to see you all dressed up."

"I like the idea," I said.

"That's what I want to hear. A confession from a true drama queen!"

Joshua rubbed his chin while eyeing me like a concerned mother.

"No, seriously. It will take my mind off Wade for a while. I need the distraction."

I explored the walk-in wardrobe, looking for ideas. I rearranged the coat hangers, expressing awe at a piece of furniture I spotted between various pieces of Viking armor.

"He's found my playpen!"

The others joined me as I stared at an enormous bed.

"It's where my harem and I sleep at night."

"How convenient," said Mannix. "The bed is right next to the costumes."

The sleeping quarters were in one major color scheme—black. The plush bedspread was darker than sin. Even with the natural light peeping in from his office, dark erotic shadows made this area a pleasure-seeker's delight. Heavy industrial lamps shone muted red tones to accentuate the lush naughty pink bits of the sole man asleep on its surface. He didn't stir, even with the murmurs of our voices.

But for all its sexual connotations, all I thought about was my husband back on Earth. I wanted to grab his hand and take him to this world, trying out this penthouse suite with only the two of us. We'd dance like lovers apart for too long, laughing together at our wayward steps. He'd try to spin me, but clumsily I'd fall onto the sheets, gazing up at the man who I once planned to spend forever with.

"Mannix, has Guy spoken to you about why it's so easy for me to visit the mortal world?"

"No, he didn't."

"Do you know why, Josh?"

"Guy and I aren't really talking yet," he replied.

"Yeah, I know, but you're of this world. Surely you have some idea why I don't need divine help to visit Wade?"

"Seriously, no. It's probably because you're a freak of nature."

"Guy told me that the answer is in your repressed memories," Mannix explained. "They'll come like pearls of wisdom when you're ready to deal with them." He looked to the charcoal ceiling. "Considering he wasn't watching you in your final days, it's a strange thing to say. Still, I'd love to know how you found a way to break the golden rule of this place. You've got me stumped." His eyes widened. "Adam, why don't you go back in time and see how you died?"

"No way," I shrieked. "I want to *remember* what happened. I don't want an eyewitness account of something I'll never forget."

"Enough about you, Adam," Preston declared. "I never finished telling you why you're putting on a play."

"Because you're oversexed."

"Nice to see you were listening, pretty boy. But there's a catch."

"A catch?"

"Well, yes. You're in the Underworld, remember? Of course there's a catch."

"And a pretty big one," Joshua interrupted. His head hung.

"Make these sinners laugh, squeal, jump out of their seats in terror, or whatever it is you thespians do, and Guy's parents will be free to leave."

"Preston, you're putting a lot of pressure on us," said Mannix. "It's like you're pimping us out, in a theater sense."

"Oh, that's such a dramatic concept." He sat on the bed, patting the spot next to him. The sleeping lad didn't stir while Mannix refused the invitation to sit. "Now, you see, if you sat next to me and rewarded me with your body, that would make me a pimp." He fondled his pearls. "No, think of this as barter. You do something for me; I do something for that dear little angel."

"Josh, you're a demon," I pleaded. "Surely both of you can come to an agreement without getting us involved. I mean, you and him, you're both from the same part of the Afterlife, aren't you?"

"Yes, Adam," he replied. "But, hey, I'm dating an angel. Preston's got a bee in his bonnet about that."

"True," our host avowed. "I need to see how deep this demon's love is. There's more at stake here than just the freedom of Guy's parents."

Josh gazed at me. His cheerless eyes made me realize that if anyone was in deep, it was him. *But to what extent?*

"We're doing it," I said. Mannix looked at me, puzzled. "Whatever else this may be about, it's primarily about a family reunion!"

Preston applauded. "Bravo. See, dramatics are in your blood."

My young friend gave our host a filthy look before turning to me with a kind smile. Joshua kissed my cheek softly and whispered thank-you.

"Whoa!" I cried. "I wasn't expecting that."

The demon sauntered away from us. Preston followed.

"Oh dear, what if we fail?"

"We won't fail," Mannix replied. "And let's not tell Guy about this. It will be a nice surprise when his parents return."

"You're right. Let's not tell him anything about it, just in case we fail."

Chapter Fourteen

"THE THINGS YOU see when you don't have a gun."

These were Wade's first words to me as he entered the Afterlife. He spat each syllable out like a piece of chewing gum. Then he kept staring as if I was supposed to remember some major event, like an alien invasion.

"Perhaps this wasn't a good idea," I replied.

"What wasn't a good idea?" he asked.

Against his better judgment, I convinced Guy to let me see Wade alone as he made his way to this side of mortality. So Guy suggested this private place. My husband stepped through the doorway of a lavish room. I stood as a lone figure on a checkered floor surrounded by ginormous red velvet curtains.

"Wade, I heard you died of a heart attack. Am I right?"

He was thinner and paler, yet the hint of silver in his short-cropped hair made him look romantically distinguished. How I wished I were three years older, just like him.

"Maude said it was a broken heart," he stated with no emotion.

"Was it me? Did I break it?"

No answer.

"Hold on, how come you remember what happened? That's not fair. I'm dealing with amnesia and you've got your memory."

Rainbow lights darted from the large chandelier above, as if rays of unseen sunlight had taken their cue to distract us. I danced as if in a disco during our courting days. Still no response. I stopped.

"I knew I shouldn't have left you alone," a voice behind me slurred.

The curtains opened as Guy stumbled toward Wade. I was relieved to see my husband take a few steps back.

"You're real!"

Guy stopped in his tracks, momentarily, then moved slower, zigzagging in Wade's direction. "Of course I'm real!"

"Are you always this drunk?" He turned to face me. "No wonder you were a mess, Adam. Your angel is an alcoholic."

"Play nice, Wade," Guy said. "We both share responsibility for what happened to Adam."

"I'm responsible?" My man looked pale. "Shit, you even have wings!"

He fluttered them. "Yes. I'm not just an imaginary childhood friend."

Wade laughed to himself, but when I met his gaze, he stopped.

"Bub, is there something I should know?" I asked.

"You died in that horrible—"

"Butterscotch or peach?" Guy inquired. He pointed to a small round table with three chairs that were not there a moment ago. On it were many small shot glasses with various-colored liquids.

"We're having schnapps?" Wade asked.

"Hold on, Guy. How come Wade remembers more than I remember?"

"He does?" His wings drooped. "You do, Wade? Oh dear. I knew I forgot something."

"Make him forget now! No. Don't. Wade, you were about to blurt out how I died."

"Wade," Guy interrupted, "Adam doesn't remember his final months."

"Months? How much amnesia have I got?"

"Oh, I see," my husband replied. "Where should we start?"

Guy gestured to the chairs so we sat. He encouraged us to try the vanilla shots.

"Where else but in the hereafter would an inebriated angel encourage you to drink," I said, in desperate need of these shots.

"Adam, you were murdered," Guy declared.

"And you were a slut," Wade added.

"You were a slut and you were murdered," Guy repeated with the subtlety of a presidential campaign. He pushed two glasses of butterscotch schnapps in my direction. I drank them fast.

"I was murdered?"

"And you were a slut," Wade repeated.

"How was I murdered?"

Guy passed two more glasses of liqueur. This time, peppermint. We took a swig. Then my angel buddy held my hand and prompted Wade to hold the other.

"What is the last memory you have of your life?" Guy asked.

"I was looking at a fantastic king-sized bed with two men in it. One of them had a chest you could crack walnuts on."

"Who was the other guy?"

"I don't remember."

"Think really hard, Adam."

I took a deep breath and closed my eyes. I could see a handsome man with a chiseled chin in the bed, but the scene was moving away from me. Like when a movie camera eases back to reveal more of the scenery. I forced myself to take a closer look. The other man came into focus.

Bald head and a goatee. It was like looking into a mirror. There I was next to Mr. Dreamboat. The sheets on top of us were soaked in blood, but somehow we looked at peace. As I studied the room, I saw more blood splattered in parallel lines up the walls and onto the ceiling. I opened my eyes to clear my head of this sickening vision.

"More schnapps, please," I said.

Guy let go of my hand and passed me a glass of banana-flavored liqueur. I drank it, then helped myself to another.

"Who killed us?" I asked, trembling.

"Trevor Murphy's stalking ex-boyfriend," said Wade.

"Who's Trevor Murphy?"

"Your one-night stand for that night."

"My one-night stand?"

"One of many." He helped himself to another glass.

"Hey, I'm the one who just confirmed I was murdered. Why do you need so much schnapps?"

"I'm just realizing I'm dead."

"What? A mammoth room that looks like it's the temple that Renaissance forgot and an angel serving us alcohol isn't enough of a clue?"

"Come on, Adam. I was in a hospital bed a moment ago. Now I'm here and the first thing I see is you. I was a bit stunned, but it's all sinking in now." He surveyed the surroundings. "I didn't think Heaven would be so opulent. Should I have been Catholic?"

"Guy, how could you forget to erase Wade's memory while I'm left struggling to piece it all together?"

"Easy, girls," he whispered. "This is supposed to be a tender reunion."

"You're avoiding the question, again."

"Look at it this way. By keeping Wade's memories intact, it will fast-forward your recovery process."

I studied the remaining glasses. I picked the red drink and the cloudy white one, and downed them fast.

"So I had a one-night stand and was killed by this guy's ex? Did I suffer?"

"I know I did," my gloomy husband remarked.

"I'm sorry, Wade."

"It was years ago, Adam."

"But you're still hurt by it. How much of a slut was I?"

"There's no time to go through the telephone book now."

"I can't have been that bad."

"You made Cleopatra look like a Girl Scout."

"But I'm not a slut at heart."

"It's not your heart that was slutting around!"

I looked to my angel. "I couldn't have been that bad, could I, Guy?"

"Well, Adam, if we need to vacuum the carpet, we could sit you down naked and drag you by the ankles. You'd suck up everything but the furniture."

"But I don't think you're sure, Guy."

"Adam, I'm your guardian angel. I know enough."

"Then why didn't you tell me before?" I poked my finger into his chest. "If you knew, then why didn't you confirm it earlier?"

He stood, and just as quickly, passed out, landing back in his chair.

"I'm sorry, Wade, I didn't know. Well, I kind of knew but can't remember any of it." Wade downed another shot and turned away. "But why? We had a great relationship. Darling, talk to me, please. I'm lost here. I really don't know what happened in my final months. I can't even believe it was months. I've been watching you privately, picking up men and going to ruin. And it's hurt me. Hurt me to know I somehow did this to you, but I don't know how. So, Wade, talk to me. What is this all about?"

"Wade, there were circumstances leading up to your fallout," my angel murmured. His eyes barely opened. "Adam can't take all the blame."

"Yeah, that's right," I said. "Guy, you mentioned that you and Wade are both responsible for what happened to me."

"When did I say that?"

"About five minutes ago."

My guardian swayed on his seat, pale as a sheet.

"I think I need to get out of here," Wade said. "It's all too much. I'm drinking with Adam and his imaginary childhood friend. But I was in the hospital a moment ago. Where was the white light? Where were the harps and the Heavenly choir? Where's God?"

He stood, looking like a fearful rabbit hiding from a fox. I got to my feet and held him. Gradually he placed an arm around me so I kissed his forehead, tasting his forgotten skin. And with a flash of light and some unrecognizable babble from Guy, Wade and I found ourselves in my apartment, holding each other.

Chapter Fifteen

"WHY HAS GUY got a boyfriend who's a demon, Adam?"

I screwed up my face, trying to think of a way to make the angel's love interest make sense. I had just told Wade about Joshua being Guy's teenage crush once upon a time. Then I told him about Guy's parents and the Underworld. All the while, we sipped peppermint tea in an effort to calm ourselves.

"It's a Heavenly soap opera, Wade."

"So we're in Heaven with an angel who's in love with someone from Hell. Geez, first you sleep around and get murdered, and now you're playing risky games with your soul. Why are we helping Guy anyway?"

"Darling, so far he's been the only constant in both my life and in my death. Plus I'm sure we'll score karma points for helping an angel, that is, if you want to help. I've seen the Underworld. I'd hate to think that by turning our backs on Guy, we'll be damned for eternity, learning how to be better cheats, liars, and thieves. Besides, the music is shit down there."

"Adam, where is God?"

"I have no idea."

He raised a brow.

"I've never heard any reference to him or her or whatever God may be. I just assumed I'll eventually find out. After all, Heaven seems like Earth. Material possessions. Homes to go to. But with an angel thrown in so we know we're no longer alive, even if he has got a drinking problem." I paused. "Maybe the Joshua thing is a test? Maybe we have to play this out to find God?"

Wade nodded calmly. "Interesting hypothesis. You've been here longer than me so I guess you know what you're talking about."

"That's just it, Wade. I'm not sure if I do. But the consequences of not doing anything may prove critical. After all, Guy's been there for me for as long as I remember."

"Maybe the easiest thing is just to tell Guy where his parents are."

"Yeah, I've thought long and hard about that. But I'm worried how Guy will react to where they are. He's protected me so many times. Now it's time for me to protect him."

I poured more tea before resting the cup against my chin, staying silent for the longest time. Laughter came from the other side of our window. I took a peek. It was Tyson who lived in the apartment next to Guy's. He still wore an idiotic knight's outfit but was stumbling, so his Maid Marion wannabe helped him to the door. Her rosy smile beamed with love. He searched his outfit frantically for the keys.

Passersby watched and shared their mirth, pointing as if this was the first drunk man they'd even seen. One young man mimicked Tyson's wayward actions before blowing a kiss to the couple. They giggled and fell to the ground.

"Wade, do you still love me?"

"Adam, I'm processing a lot here."

"It's a simple question."

"I'll always love you."

"But are you in love with me?"

He pursed his lips before sipping his tea.

"Tell me what happened in those final days."

"Final days? Adam, things began falling apart months before I lost you."

"Go on. I have all the time in the world to hear this story."

"You went weird."

"Weird? How weird? Playing dress-ups weird? Getting fat weird? Finding a new religion weird?"

"Um."

"What? Finding a new religion weird? What weird religion did I find?"

"Not interfaith, that's for sure."

"What was I doing? Chanting all day and night? Sacrificing small children? Praying for a sign?"

"Praying, no. But you were on your knees a lot." He smiled at his own humor. "Adam, it's not your cosmic aspects that upset me. It was your constant sleeping around."

"Who was Trevor Murphy?"

"The last one of many. At first, I thought you couldn't handle Mannix's death, but then you went on and on finding sex like an addict."

"I don't remember."

"I don't care if you remember, Adam. I remember! That's what hurts."

I tried to put my hand on his shoulder, but he pushed it away.

"Can you even consider how lonely it is to lie awake in bed night after night, wondering if your husband is coming home? Can you even imagine the pain I felt as the clock ticked way past midnight and you still weren't in our bed?"

"Wade..."

"No, Adam, listen. At first, I found out about your mystery lovers through Maude. She kept it from me at first, but when there was more than one, she felt it her duty to tell me. But what difference did it make? You were hardly home. And when you did come home all smug, you weren't really there as my husband." He stood.

So did I. "Wade, I don't remember any of this, but I do remember your secret dalliance with Mannix."

"Something that pales in comparison to the slut you became!"

"Wade, I'm serious. I don't remember. As far as I'm concerned, we were still in a loving relationship."

"Loving? You call us a loving relationship? The first one was Bill. Then there was that couple that looked like they were both dropped on their heads at birth. Oh, and that fetus with the sports car. What he saw in an old fart like you, I'll never know. Was Alfie next, or was it, Steve? It was Steve, because he bought you that ridiculous bracelet, thinking you were in love with him. You, of all people. Do you even know the meaning?"

"How dare you! I loved you, Wade, since the first time I laid eyes on you. I've been your partner in crime through my twenties, thirties, and some of my forties—and you dare question my love for you! Since I've been here alone, all I've thought about is being with you. I snuck down to Earth a few times just to see you."

"And I've spent three years trying to get over you, and once I did, there you were in front of me in this loony bin!"

"After three years, that should have been a happy moment."

"Trust me, Adam, it wasn't!"

"Oh, I'm seeing a clear picture now. Mannix. One-night stands. And a boy young enough to be your son, happy that you passed out. Don't worry, Wade, I saw it all. Without me, you became a loser!"

"Better being a loser than a flaky no one."

"Flaky?"

"Yes, flaky! Like a helium balloon that was let go of. Getting higher and higher until it was no use to anyone. Not me. And not to the hordes who used you to hide their loneliness."

"If I was ever the slut you claim I was, then maybe I had a good reason."

"Yeah, so you could abandon me like the way your father abandoned his family!"

"Time out, guys," Guy yelled as he charged through our front door. "You've gone off the rails."

He handed me a handkerchief to wipe my eyes. I huffed to soothe my nerves, but it was a fruitless task.

"How could you forget to erase Wade's memory? He's got the advantage. This should be a loving reunion."

"There's a lot for you to discuss, isn't there, Wade?" Guy said in a low tone.

My husband shook visibly in anger.

"There are two sides to every story, isn't there, Wade?"

"Not from my perspective," he answered.

"I don't know what's going on," I said. "For one thing, Guy, you're supposed to be *my* guardian angel. Yet here you've left me alone with my demonic husband like it's some kind of cruel joke. And you, my snarky little Wade, as far as I'm concerned, we loved each other. And I don't know who those men you mentioned were..."

I paused again.

"What is it?" Guy asked.

"Nothing."

Outside our window, beings merely existed. They had no script or reason for their actions. Not even Tyson and his girlfriend had meaning. They were players in the backdrop of this silly drama. And I didn't need any of this. I stood, went to the bedroom, and grabbed a coat, then made sure the front door slammed on my way out.

Chapter Sixteen

THERE'S SOMETHING THERAPEUTIC about boredom. Droning lecturers introduced me to the hundred and one ways you can hold a pen, and the many types of personalities a person named Peter can have. And all this with little input expected from me.

And I never realized what a beautiful color gray could be. It acts as a canvas for my mind to project my dramas onto, over and over, until they no longer matter.

Decisions were made for me. When to eat. When to sleep. And now and again Preston would amble through the corridors like a shooting star. In anyone else, this understated charisma was seldom obtainable. Yet this pearl-wearing man never merely entered a room; he quietly commanded it with the ease of a champion figure skater whose hypnotic moves are never unnoticed.

Yet his brand of magnetism was too much effort to aim for. I was just a human, merely being, and it was peaceful.

And for some reason during my time here, Guy's parents had never crossed my path. I admit I didn't go actively searching, but I assumed that an older couple with wings wouldn't be too hard to spot.

"Here you go." Mary handed me something with bits of greenery I assumed was coriander. Either that or it was continental parsley. It tasted like neither.

"Thank you," I replied. "I still don't understand why you ended up here."

The short Christian took a mouthful, chewing with her jaw circling itself like a cow eating grass.

"It reminds me of home."

"This is what your home is like? Hmm. Peaceful."

"You're starting to understand me, Adam."

"Perhaps."

"You see, here I don't need to make decisions. I follow the flock."

"Did it ever occur to you to stand out at home?"

"My husband spoke, and it was my job to agree. And he had plenty of opinions. Opinions on city folk. Opinions on our congregation. Opinions on hardening up the kids."

"And you never had opinions of your own?"

She nodded.

"I'm seeing how peaceful life is when you don't have an opinion."

A tear glistened as it made a track down her cheek. It was something different to notice. But I didn't want different. I didn't want my mind to activate; otherwise it wouldn't shut off and Wade would haunt me even further. I looked at my food. It wasn't different, so I ate another mouthful.

"I wanted opinions," she murmured. "God didn't bless me with any."

A second spoonful of blandness made it to my lips, but it was too late; my mind was ticking over. "Mary, you have misguided *opinions* on homosexuals."

"And it was my husband's opinion that our little Toby was too soft." I studied her without letting expression show on my face. She was disturbing my peace, and I was getting drawn in like a fish losing the battle with a fisherman.

"And was Toby...?"

"Yes, Toby was a fairy!"

She looked into space; quiet for the longest time. I ate, watching her and waiting for her to continue.

"I suppose you think I'm a horrible mom."

"I don't have an opinion, Mary. Well, not yet, anyway."

"He kept playing with dolls. His sister's dolls. My husband would smack him every time he discovered Toby with those dolls. In the end, I buried those dolls so Toby would never be struck by my husband again."

"But they were your *daughter*'s dolls."

"And Cindy cried for a week."

"What did she play with instead?"

"The sticks and stones around the creek where we lived."

I looked to my food again, as an escape from this unsettling story. Mary took a mouthful herself but choked as she tried to swallow. I jumped up and thumped her back, hard. She coughed, finally spitting out the unclassifiable cuisine.

We sat, staring at each other for a while. Her soul was indefinable. The ghostly shell of a woman who was once so full of hate had achieved the numbness I was after. But her story was penetrating the layers of my brain I was using to shut her out.

"What toys did Toby have?"

"My husband and I saved for months, then waited for the post-Christmas sales to buy a racing car set for him and new dolls for our daughter. But we had spawned a devil child, and we had to take temptation away from him."

"I have a strong feeling that the dolls were not the end of Toby's interests."

"He'd dance. He'd dance all the time. We stopped putting the damn radio on so my husband wouldn't have to watch him dance. He'd call him a mommy's boy and wonder what we did wrong to deserve a fate like this."

"Your son left as soon as he was old enough to leave home, didn't he, Mary?"

"Our son never…" She swallowed hard. "That God-forsaken sinner never did leave home. I would hear him sing out from the creek to me, from time to time. His voice like an angel telling me he forgave me."

She sat perfectly still as her eyes wandered around the room, not focusing on any one thing. I felt my stomach drop through the floor as she hummed a cheerful tune through emotionless lips.

"Mary, what happened to Toby?"

"It was one of those cool nights. You know, too cold for the mosquitoes to bite and not warm enough to have *too* many people over. So my husband asked Peggy-Sue and Bob around for dinner. They were our neighbors." Mary paused as if she was waiting for the scene to unfold before her eyes. "I never liked Peggy-Sue. I don't know why. No. That's not true. I do know why."

She met my gaze. "Peggy-Sue was opinionated like my husband. Maybe even more so. They agreed about so much. They'd run down the government of the time, whoever was in power. Bob and I were often on the outer when we all got together, keeping our opinions to ourselves. On this particular night, it was cool."

"Yes, you already said."

"I don't know why he always did this to me."

"Did what, Mary? Did what?"

"I had all the time in the world, but he'd send me out for groceries as our guests arrived. It happened time and time again. Guests would show up, and I'd never have enough food. So they'd arrive, and he'd entertain them without me."

"Did Peggy-Sue arrive before Bob on this particular night?"

Her lips clenched.

"So Peggy-Sue, your husband, and your kids were at home. No, hold on. You probably took the kids shopping."

She shook her head. "No. I usually do, but this time I wanted the kids to stay with him."

"And Peggy-Sue?"

"He said it was an accident. Peggy-Sue confirmed his story. Bob didn't come home from work until after it happened. But Cindy's face said it all."

Mary trembled like a dog left out in the cold.

"I'm so scared to ask this, but what happened?"

"In time, I left my husband. I ran into the arms of Bob and we moved upstate. Peggy-Sue never wanted Cindy. But Cindy wasn't being a good Christian child. Black nail polish and lipstick were her thing. I heard she died of an overdose after she ran away from home."

"Mary, what happened to Toby that cool night?"

"The police confirmed it was an accident. I mean, eight-year-old boys are prone to drowning. They spoke to my husband because I was no use. I wasn't there when it happened. It was an open-and-shut case as far as the police were concerned."

"Mary, I'm so sorry."

"Whatever for? My fairy boy drowned that night. God took him to make him into a man."

"Oh dear Mary." I fell back in my chair and covered my mouth.

"I know God took him. He'd sing to me from the creek to let me know he was okay. Somewhere here I'll find him one day, and he'll be big and strong like a man should be. He'll hold his mother in his arms and forgive me for not being there that night."

I felt ill. I staggered out of my chair, knocking it over as I stood. I held my gut and convinced myself not to throw up. I ran out of that room and into another. There were people in that room so I kept going. Until there it was. My spot. A corner with no one around.

I sat, clutching my arms around my knees and rocked back and forth for a reason I couldn't fathom. Too many thoughts were entering my head. I tried to push them out. Really, I tried.

How could Mary be so deluded? How could anyone treat their homosexual son like they were an abomination? What barbaric times did she live in?

I closed my eyes and strained every muscle to keep still. I was here, away from a husband who hated me. The very person who could hold me right now and ease my horror. But he'd never love me again after what I apparently did.

But how could my dramas even compare to what Mary thought about her own son?

I finally sat still, never wanting to feel anything again.

Chapter Seventeen

"I HAD A hunch you'd be here, Adam."

I looked up from my tasteless porridge. Each time I had it, I imagined it contained any number of delicious fruit. Today I picked blueberries as my fantasy additive.

"Josh, I really want to be alone."

"Guy's been worried sick about you. And so has someone else."

"I don't care. I need this reboot, or this escape, or whatever the Underworld is supposed to be about."

"Is it working?"

"I'm finding out so much. Did you realize whichever side of the road you drive your car on, which totally depends on which country you're in, is the same side of the pavement you walk on?"

"No, Adam, but I'm riveted."

"So was I. You see, if you drive on the left like me, you'll naturally walk on the left of the pavement. And if you drive on the—"

"Stop. It was sarcasm. You know me. You should have picked up on it."

"And that's why I'm here. I'm sick of being slapped down and hearing about other people who've been slapped down." I lowered my eyes and kept eating.

"Adam, um…"

"Josh, if you have nothing to say to me, then please, leave me alone."

"How about a game of cards?"

"Why? And why are you trying to bond with me?"

"Even a demon has wisdom to share."

"In fifteen minutes, there's a talk on the Delight of Premolars. I don't want to miss it."

"Adam, they're teeth. How exciting can they be?"

I opened my mouth and pointed. "They're in here somewhere, and I want to know their function."

Joshua turned away like a forgotten pet, finally leaving me in peace. Soon after, a couple of ants came crawling onto my table. Somehow they knew not to go near my breakfast, but I spooned a drop onto the surface for them to indulge in.

They had a smaller world than mine, and I was envious. I still had a choice about the lectures I attended. They didn't have that freedom. They searched for food or did whatever ants are supposed to do at the time they had to do it. I wanted to be caged up in an ant hole and forgotten.

The image of a man in a crown with a red triangle at his side encroached upon my peripheral vision.

"I said I didn't want to play cards, Josh."

"Humor me."

The ace of spades made an appearance, followed by the two of hearts and a whole series of numbers and suits from the quickly laid-out deck.

"What do you want to play?"

"Poker, of course. What other game would an Underworld figure play?"

"What if I lose? Do you take my soul?"

"If only. No, that would be something Preston would take. Not me."

He picked up the deck and shuffled, then swiftly laid five cards in front of us both. I picked up my hand and surprisingly discovered three aces. Joshua threw away three cards as I tried to stop from grinning.

"Why are you here with me instead of spending time with Guy?"

"Because you're important to Guy, who in turn is important to me. Plus I need you." He passed two new cards to me. "Adam, can I ask you an unrelated question?"

"Sure."

"Has Preston made a pass at you since you've been here?"

"I keep in the shadows, Josh. I don't want to break anyone's heart." I showed my three aces proudly as my poker partner had nothing but two sevens. He dealt again. "But the strange thing is. Mary's here."

"I know. I've seen her. She's come to terms with my demon form."

"She probably believes she's in purgatory."

"How long are you planning to stay here, Adam?"

"I see no reason to leave. I mean, at least I'll already be here to put on the play, if that's what you're worried about."

"No, that's not what I'm worried about."

I picked up my hand. Two queens. Two jacks. I threw one card back. So did he.

"Josh, can I ask you a question?"

"Shoot."

"Are you sure? It's personal."

"No, it's fine. Ask the question."

"You once said to me that you learned to be blunt during your childhood. Why?"

He laid his cards on the table. Four aces. Incredible luck. I showed my hand before he shuffled again and dealt.

"Because my parents didn't communicate, so I did their communicating for them."

I left the cards untouched.

"They never said they loved each other, so I said it for them, even when they tried to talk over me."

"I think we had similar childhoods."

"And when I tried to be louder, nothing changed. So I kept quiet for a while until I learned the power of bluntness. It cuts through when politeness is ignored. It shakes the listener and makes them wake up from their delusions. It sounds like bad karma, but it's a message that needs to be taken in."

"Or it's a way to keep perspective on the world around you." I heard his heart deflate. "Josh, when your parents talked over you, what did they say?"

"Dreams fade in time. Reality sets in. Childhood doesn't last forever."

"But did they ever say love is lost?"

"No, not exactly."

"So there was still hope in their hearts. A quest to find the missing passion."

"Adam, are we talking about your parents or mine?"

"You're being blunt again. And I'm right. Your bluntness is to keep the sense of the world you've built around yourself."

"So my bluntness is a security blanket?"

"I'm not saying there's anything wrong with that. We all need our armor."

For the first time in days, warmth filled me. He shook his head and returned the smile I hadn't realized I revealed. I picked up the cards he had already dealt. I kept the king of hearts and threw down the rest. He kept two cards.

"Let's talk about you, Adam."

I nodded.

"Why did you pick the Underworld to escape to?"

"There's space for an echo here. I needed to hear my thoughts."

"You're sounding melancholy." Three aces again, and the king of spades. Odd. "And, Adam, melancholy is an emotion for dreamers."

"No it's not, Josh. It's the moment where everything balances. All your emotions and thoughts stay in a temporary state of stillness. They don't battle each other. They don't cloud each other's messages. They just are. They make themselves felt in equal measure, all at the same time."

"You can't stay in that mood forever."

"I've mastered it to perfection after talking to Mary. Feeling no pain is its own reward."

"Like I said, it's an emotion you can't cling onto, my friend."

"Your friend? I never thought I'd hear the day you called me your friend, Josh." I peered down my nose. "Show me your cards."

He had two sevens but nothing else. I laid my cards down.

"Remarkable. You're better at this than I am. Another hand, or do you have to go to that talk on teeth?"

"Another hand, please."

He shuffled and dealt again. "So you're enjoying my company, Adam?"

Three jacks. He replaced two of my cards and two of his own.

"Well, I'm not exactly bored."

"So when are you returning to Wade?"

"I haven't decided." I was about to show my cards but changed my mind. "He hates me."

"For real hate to exist, real love had to preexist."

"It's funny. I've heard David say that before."

"So I'm not the only one with wisdom."

"All the same, Wade's not my number-one fan. Why are you looking at me like that?"

"There's a knowing in your voice."

"A what?"

I showed my three jacks. Joshua only had a two, a three, and a five of hearts. He didn't pay attention to my hand.

"You've remembered your past. That's what I mean by a 'knowing in your voice,' Adam."

"You're speculating."

"Oh, no, I'm not."

My eyes darted around the room.

"I'm a demon. Share the delicious details, Adam. Who were these men?"

"Look. My hand beats yours. I had three jacks."

"And I bet you had more than three jacks in your final months."

"You're being blunt again."

"Adam, seriously, you need to talk. We're alone. Who were these men?" He gathered up our cards and put the deck aside. "I promise I'll listen and not say anything."

"All right. I remember Trevor Murphy clearly, and some of the others not so clearly. And I have a feeling I met them all at the same place. Or through each other, but originally from the same place. I just don't know what that place was."

"Go on."

"Trevor seemed to know me well. We were intimate, but exactly what we did is a mystery to me. After all, we couldn't have had sex. I was in love with Wade."

"Let's get back to Trevor."

"Wade was being cold to me, but that's probably because I was sleeping around."

"Adam, the topic is Trevor."

"I thought you weren't going to interrupt."

"Trust me, I'm listening. I'm listening to the subtext."

"Trevor was a fun guy, and I remember he was trying to convince me to patch things up with Wade. I remember the conversation before we had—"

"Typical male. Tells you to go back to your husband but still has sex with you. Sorry, Adam, go on."

"But that's the thing, Josh. I don't remember having sex with him. I feel we were naked, but..." I sighed. "And I told him how distant Wade had become, but Trevor believed in true love. So did his ex. That was the last conversation I had with anyone before I arrived here in the Afterlife."

"Is that all you remember?"

"If you're asking me about my murder, well, no, not really. Just impressions and ghastly images as I left my body."

Joshua shuffled the cards again, then laid them down to the side. "It seems like Trevor had good advice."

"I guess."

"Oh, sorry, Adam. You're late for your molars talk."

"Premolars, Josh. It's a talk about premolars."

"Well, if you miss that one, there's a never-to-be-repeated lecture titled 'Doorbells of the World.' Which one rings your bell?'"

I stood. "How are you and Guy doing?"

"He's still hesitant to talk to me, even if he did ask if you were here."

"When we drag him here, it will be different. He might even sober up."

"Only if he trusts me enough to follow me back here."

"Once he knows his parents are here, you won't be able to keep him away."

"Yes, but an angel in the Underworld? You can see why I negotiated heavily with Preston."

"Wouldn't an angel's light be stronger than any of Preston's tricks?"

Josh bit his bottom lip.

"Maybe not. Anyway, I put in a good word for you with Guy."

He grinned. "Thank you, Adam."

"No, thank you, Josh. I needed our talk. Plus I'm feeling curiously empowered. I suspect it's because you let me win at cards so often."

"I'm neither going to deny nor admit to your accusation, Adam."

I smiled gently. "And gray is a color I don't want to see for a while."

"So, can I walk you out?"

"Not just yet. It's time to meet Guy's parents. Will you take me to them?"

"No."

"No? Why not?"

"I promised Preston I wouldn't interfere with your stay here, and if he sees us together, he'll know I broke that promise."

"Really? Why didn't he want you to talk to me?"

"Adam, there's more to my deal with him than I can say. Just trust me. I know what I'm doing."

"Wow, this guy really has you under his thumb."

"More than you realize. But now you have to promise *me* something."

I nodded.

"When you see them, don't try to exit with them."

"Why not?"

"Because an angel's exit from the Underworld is a little more complicated than a human's."

"More riddles?"

"More riddles." He took my hand. "I'm surprised you never met them. You were eating porridge a moment ago. You would have seen them in the kitchen."

"Why? Are they on cooking duty?"

"They're always on cooking duty. It's their favorite role."

"But they can't cook!"

"And they never improve. You must have seen them when you needed food."

"I didn't go to the kitchen. Mary kept bringing me my meals."

"Of course. She found more angels to talk to, and they found another hopeless case to try to help."

"Well, I can't leave without meeting them."

He clutched my hand tighter. "Adam, listen to me carefully. The longer you're here, the longer you'll stay, and I don't want you to stay. It's unhealthy. So after you meet them, make sure you leave straight away!"

Chapter Eighteen

I LEFT JOSHUA and marched in the direction of the kitchen, making my way through several conference rooms.

"Hey, you there!"

I spun on my feet.

"Who me?"

"Yes, you."

A tall thin man in a beige waistcoat pointed a cane at me. His other hand sat on his waist, resembling the kind of schoolteacher from an era when kids used to be violently disciplined. His curly locks were the color of a freshly picked carrot, and his heavily freckled face gave me the inclination to find a pen and join the dots.

"I don't like stragglers who come to my talks late!"

"I was only shooting through."

He whacked his cane on the outdated blackboard behind him. "No one shoots through my talks." His vicious stick pointed to a spare chair near me. "Now sit!"

"No, really, I didn't plan on sitting in on your talk, whatever your talk is about."

"The gentle art of persuasion."

"Yeah, but I think I know everything I need to know about that subject."

"It's about sex."

I sat. Guy's parents could wait.

"Now where was I up to before the rude interruption?"

"Creating a social occasion for romance," replied a woman with a lazy eye.

"Thank you." He picked up a piece of white chalk and wrote the word *jealousy* on the board. "This is the key ingredient to getting the object of your desire into your love chamber."

I stared inanely at the word. "What does a social occasion have to do with jealousy?"

"Did I ask for questions?"

"This is a lesson. Questions are always asked during a lesson."

He whipped his cane on an empty chair in the front row. Those around the seat jumped out of their skin.

"You are a little upstart, aren't you?"

I stood. "What is your problem? I asked you a question, and as the teacher, you should answer it. That's how school worked when I was young."

"Well, judging by your shaved head and beard, you are definitely not from my era. And in my era, students listened."

What a wanker! He was a man in search of power rather than respect. I sat.

"Now, is anyone else confused by how creating jealousy can woo a beauty to your bed?"

Everyone raised their hand.

"Very well. The secret is in making yourself seem popular. You must make a list of those who have sent you perfumed love letters, small gifts, and for the ladies, a marriage proposal, and make sure these people are free for your gathering."

"That's sick," I murmured to myself.

"Did I hear something?" He stared at me like a serial killer.

"Not from me."

He continued eyeing me momentarily. "So, your potential lover will want to be at your side during your exclusive event, but keep shy of them. Flirt with the others. Make them all think they have a chance."

"That's sick," said a woman with hair that resembled a bad wig.

"That's what I thought," I replied.

"Well, it looks like impoliteness is a trend." He strode up to her. "So why do you feel that a social gathering of such significance would make you feel ill?"

She stood while straightening the shoulders of her gray shirt.

"If I was invited to a party where the host ignored me, and I found out that various love interests were the other guests, I'd slap that man into tomorrow."

"Really, my dear. You haven't grasped the total concept of my courting method. I assure you that by listening without interruption, I can change your view."

She sat, guardedly. The orange-haired lecturer made his way back to the blackboard.

"Loser," I whispered. The woman turned and winked at me.

"Now the real trick is to make sure you don't come off like a loser." He glared at me before drawing four stick figures. "This one here is you, the host. The one over here is your love interest. Let's call her Penelope. Make sure that before the event that will be known as the social of the year, you treat Penelope to a scrumptious three-course dinner."

There was a general drone around the room.

"Glad most of you are paying attention. Wine and dine Penelope, making sure you drop in a story of your unhappy boyhood, your one true love who didn't love you back, and the wonderful career that gives you lots of money yet no time to spend it with that special someone. Lie if you have to."

I grunted.

"Sorry, what was that?" He held his hand to his ear. "Do you have more experience in this regard?"

"I have experience in love," I said.

"Then you should understand my method."

"Oh, I'm following your method. It's opening my eyes."

"Good, then I can continue with my talk." His cane pointed to one of the other stick figures. "And here we have your major weapon. Whatever you do, make sure your most high-profile admirer is at your function. Let's call her Catherine. Catherine comes from breeding. She expects everything she wants. But you are the lover she cannot have. You've flirted with her on occasion. And she believes there is no contest for your affection."

"Hold on," I said. I stood while briefly making eye contact with the woman whose hairstyle was a crime. "If Catherine comes from breeding, and a man like yourself possibly doesn't—"

"I'm appalled at your remark."

"No, listen. I mean hypothetically. Surely if there's a woman with money who wants you, wouldn't it be better to just court her?"

"But what about love?" the woman questioned.

"This isn't a talk about love. It's about getting Penelope into bed and potentially breaking her heart."

"True. This teacher is just in it for the sex."

"I'm in it for the courtship," he asserted.

"Really?" I replied. "But you're saying throw a party so you can get everyone you're being deceitful to in one room and play with their hearts."

"It's not the way I'd phrase it."

"It's the way it sounded."

"Please! Sit down and let me finish."

I did.

He pointed at the last figure on the blackboard. "And here is Cecilia. Poor Cecilia. Life has not taught her simple social graces. She's awkward around men. She prefers the company of her pet poodle rather than socializing with her siblings—"

"Oh brother!" My fellow disruptive student spoke again. All eyes were on her.

"What's the matter this time? Do you identify with Cecilia?"

She stood. "Okay, I don't know where you got the idea you were a Casanova, but your talk is bordering on misogyny."

His hand spread over his chest. "Me? Misogynistic? I guess that is something that the fairer sex would say."

"Fairer sex, my ass!"

He walloped the empty chair again with his cane. When she didn't sit, he hit it again. She shook her head and lowered herself.

"Now, the reason for Cecilia is that she is there to make Penelope feel superior. And the reason we have such a celebrated socialite like Catherine at the shindig is to make Penelope feel what?" His hand sat behind his ear again. "Come on, pupils, the word is on the board. Do I need to spoon-feed you?"

He rolled his eyes as his cane hit the emotion he'd written on the board.

"Jealousy," muttered the others with the enthusiasm of a waiter working a double shift.

"Precisely. Now, this is the delicious part. You will have entertainment better than vaudeville. And your manhood will never be questioned in polite society as Penelope works on Cecelia to make her feel ever more inferior."

I cringed.

"It will start out as idle chitchat, I assure you, but what will happen is that a game of champions will be held."

I jumped out of my seat. "You're proposing a fight."

"No. I'm proposing an argument, but if fisticuffs are a result, then all the more reason to shame poor Cecelia and take Penelope's side."

"Mate, you need a reality check."

The woman, whose hair fashion forgot, rose again. "I agree," she said. "You need a reality check. On what planet would Penelope make waves by trying to win your heart by fighting with another guest?"

"And seriously," I added, "how would a 'lady of breeding' like Catherine ever think your party is the party to end all parties, when everyone's shouting and screaming?"

"It's chivalry. I escort Cecelia out, clutching her hand while consoling her lost heart—"

"Wait a second," said my fellow rebel rouser. "You were going to shame her a moment ago. Now you're going all sweet on her. Make up your mind."

"No. You see I'd shame her in front of Penelope, then escort her out like a true gentleman."

"To use your language, you'd escort her out like a cad, and everyone at that party would see your true colors."

"My intentions are as noble as any other man of my century."

"I'd argue that," I said.

"Do you know many men from the nineteenth century?"

"I know enough about men in general to know that there's not a noble bone in your body."

Quiet murmurs filled the room. Once again, this excuse for a teacher headed my way.

"And how do you gauge a man?"

"The same way I gauge anyone, man or woman or someone in between."

"Well, enlighten us all."

"It's the way they tend to matters of the heart. It's the way they make those they love feel like they're the most important person talking when they have something to say. It's about being there when life isn't quite what they expected it to be, and showing them that what they have is better than what they think they deserve." I swallowed. "It's about never betraying the trust of the most important people, or person, in your life." I looked at my feet. My dull gray shoes were as lifeless as I felt. I sat.

"So poetic. But that's not the way to win affection."

"I think it's exactly how to win affection," the weird-haired woman said.

He sidled up to her. "Game playing is an art."

"In your case, the chess pieces are smarter than the player."

"Were you a spinster in your last life?"

Whack! She slapped him.

He patted his red cheek. Applause filled the room. He ran back to the blackboard and thrashed the life out of it with his cane, but no one paid attention. They laughed and chatted while his voice screamed for attention. He bounced up onto the empty seat in the front row and began to remove his vest. His crisp white shirt was then flung to the floor. The cane broke in two as it was thrown against the board, yet its snap was hardly heard.

Joshua ran into the room as the lecturer beat his chest like some oversized beast about to scale the Empire State Building. Then he struck the pose of a bare-fisted boxer. I couldn't help laugh as my demon friend grabbed my hand and escorted me out of the room.

"What happened?" he asked.

"Not everyone agreed with what he had to say."

"I knew his topic was too interesting for this place."

"Interesting? I'd rather listen to the talk on teeth than have to sit through that again."

"Why didn't you just go to the kitchen to see Guy's parents?"

"I got distracted." I halted, causing Josh to pull on my arm harder. "Let's go and see them now."

"No. I've got to get you out of here before Preston knows what's happened."

"He really has got you wrapped around his little finger."

He jerked me forward and I stumbled to keep up with him. After several rooms, we made it past the faceless men and women who were learning about the pear and its importance in Denmark. Then we were with Preston's youthful harem who boogied around their record machine as I cheerfully ambled up to the sleaziest one and kissed him on the lips.

After our mouths parted, he ran his finger down my cheek and I stepped away from his cage. Joshua clutched my hand again and marched me to the base of the stairs leading to the exit.

"You took me away from these boys pretty fast. Were you saving my soul?"

"Adam, I already have."

"More riddles?"

"More riddles."

I climbed the steps toward the manhole cover but stopped when I realized my demon friend was still at its base.

"Aren't you coming with me? Oh. You're avoiding Guy."

He waved me up the ladder. I continued, carefully opening the manhole and climbing out. As I turned to place the cover back, two sets of eyes held my gaze against the night sky.

Chapter Nineteen

"GUY. WADE. WHAT are you doing here?"

"Adam, more importantly, what were you doing in the Underworld?" the angel asked. "In fact, how did you even know that place existed? That's no place for you!"

He took the manhole cover from my hands and slammed it into place. Then in an instant, he had a champagne bottle in his hand, while Wade suddenly held a tray with three empty glasses.

"I can always rely on you for a festive mood, Guy."

"You shouldn't have been down there," Wade scolded through gritted teeth.

"It looks like you've had time to get to know each other," I said.

"And we both share a concern for you," Guy admitted.

"A common cause can start a conversation," said Wade. "Besides, what else is someone new to the Afterlife supposed to do?"

"Was I the only topic of conversation?"

Guy nodded, then poured our drinks.

"Pity." My glass was about to wet my lips. "Hey, hold on a second. Wade, you're talking to me. What's changed?"

He looked to my guardian and then back to me.

"I've been sorting Wade out since you disappeared. And now that you're back where you should be, I have to sort you out as well."

"Guy, I'm sorry I went off at you."

"Adam, I'm an angel dealing with people's issues all day. I have a few battle scars already. Your outburst was an annoying insect bite compared to what else I've been put through."

Wade moved to my guardian's side.

"And did you really think you'd find answers in the Underworld? Besides, look what they dressed you in. Gray pajamas! It's hardly the height of fashion." He snapped his fingers. A smart jacket, a scarf, and jeans that were a bit young for me adorned my body. "That's better. Traveling clothes."

"Where are we going?"

"On a secret adventure, apparently," Wade replied.

"What?"

"That's all he told me."

"Yes, my guardian angel likes to talk in riddles."

"Now listen," Guy said, "This is the first of three locations I need to take you to."

As he spoke, the entrance to the Underworld was replaced by something entirely unexpected. My own funeral.

"Who are those men?" I inquired. "The ones grouped in the middle?" I pointed. "The ones with that toy rabbit dressed in black."

Wade grunted, then asked, "You don't remember?"

"Are you sure you don't remember, Adam?" Guy probed. "Do any of those faces look familiar?"

"This would be a lot easier if you gave me my memory back," I replied.

"I'm already skating on thin ice. I can't make the same mistake twice." He gulped half of his champagne.

"Do you want me to remember, Wade?"

"I want to feel better about our relationship. I don't care how we get there."

Everything faded before a scene in a cemetery took its place. There was a younger version of my husband chatting to our good friend, Maude. They stood apart from the others who were watching my casket slowly lower into my final resting place.

"Oh, this conversation." Wade trailed off on the last word.

I felt tense, so I knocked back my whole glass of bubbly.

"I'm proud of you, Wade," Maude began. "You said nothing about Adam's adventures in your elegy."

"I'd never stoop that low."

"And what you said was so..." She swallowed hard. "Forgive me."

"Cry if you need to."

"No, I need to say this. Your elegy was very moving. A testament to the love you had."

"Yes, the love we *had*."

"Wade, I still don't believe for one minute that Adam slept with all those men."

"And I had to see them while I delivered my eulogy. Besides, you were the one who first told me, Maude."

"I told you as much as I knew. I didn't say that Adam—"

"They like to get naked. What else—"

"Yes, you've said. But ignore the gossip and the rest is just hearsay. I really think you've become so obsessed with a little infidelity that you can't see past what you both had."

"A *little* infidelity."

"You stopped respecting him a while ago. Can you really expect..."

At first it wasn't clear why Maude stopped midsentence. We heard shoes making that thud sound they do on grass. Behind us others were coming to see why my husband and our best friend were arguing.

This scene faded, and with our glasses magically topped back up with champagne, another funeral appeared.

"Hold on," I said. "I want to know what else you talked about. Maude was arguing in my defense."

"We never brought up the subject again," my husband replied. "We hardly spoke again after that."

I was about to tell him I knew. That I had heard her attempts to contact him on a vintage answering machine. But for some reason, I didn't.

Maude appeared again, slimmer than she was at my funeral, and obviously much sadder. She had moved away from where Wade's coffin was being lowered and reached for a small daisy that had sprung up through the grass. She smelled it, then kissed it.

"A token of love to my two dearest friends. May you both rest in peace. May you both find joy, and..." She laughed to herself. "And Guy, if you really do exist, help Wade and Adam fall in love again."

"Of course you had to show us that," I groaned. "A new member of the Guy Appreciation Club, even though Maude's never seen you. Or has she?"

The angel shook his head. "I'm just showing you that others believe in your love."

"More than I do at the moment." Wade didn't sound sarcastic when these words slipped out. Truth be told, I wasn't sure what his mood was.

The winged one snapped his fingers again. Both my husband and I had woolen beanies clutched to our bald scalps.

"It's a cold night," Guy said. "You both need to keep warm."

"But it wasn't cold a moment ago," I replied. "Perhaps we need hot chocolate instead of, hey, hold on, what happened to our champagne?"

"No, Adam. The journey we're going on will astonish you. I don't need my lovebirds spilling drinks with their mouths agape."

Guy held our hands as into the darkness we rose. We were enchanted astronauts without a rocket. The stars blazed with their thousand watchful eyes, keeping our flight safe. Yet it was the moon we were aiming for. Its crescent shape shimmered like a waterfall, and as we got nearer, droplets fell on our faces.

"Aren't you worried we'll catch a cold, Guy?" Wade asked. "I mean, the droplets on our faces can't be good for us." The sprinkle became a light shower.

"Close your eyes, gentlemen," he instructed. "I know what I'm doing."

I'm not sure what my husband did, but I definitely closed my eyes. The water formed into liquid hands, which massaged my body, and as I relaxed, I was compelled to speak:

"In another life we were paupers.
I fell ill.
You held me tight.
I died too soon."

"What did you say, Adam?" my husband asked.

"I'm not sure. It's a poem I once heard."

I opened my eyes. We stood on the tip of the moon's pointy edge, but it wasn't the moon anymore. It was a rosewood floor cut to a protruding angle, suspended in space, surrounded by darkness. And rain was falling as we huddled under black umbrellas.

A spotlight came on and lit two figures in the shadows by our side. A woman with eyes as dark as ravens, shivered with a lifeless man in her arms.

"That's us," Wade said. "I know it is."

"How do you know?" I asked.

"I know what your eyes look like when they're sad."

"But didn't I just recite that 'I fell ill'? Aren't I the one dead in *her* arms?"

"The poem is from the man's perspective," Guy replied. "Just because you remembered the poem doesn't mean it can't be from Wade's perspective."

"Oh dear, look at my sorrow. I've lost my true love."

"Yet we're both so young," my husband noted.

"And in that life, Adam, or Autumn as you were known then, lived for another twenty years," Guy explained. The young woman grew older in front of our eyes. Her face smeared with a lonely expression. "And in that life you never remarried."

"Didn't I long for companionship?" I asked.

"Oh, Adam, you had lovers. You even had a serious one much later in life. But he wasn't your soul mate."

"It explains the sad face," Wade added. "See, you're lost without me."

"Well, there's a boost for your ego," I joked.

The rain stopped, and our umbrellas faded to nothing. We were oddly dry as well. The light faded on Autumn as the sun lit a scene on the opposite side.

A gentle lass picked flowers in an expansive garden. Her green eyes stared as if her soul had diminished long before this point in time. And there was the likeness of me, looking out from a castle big enough to house a village. But the version of me soon lost interest, as the woman sat on the ground weeping.

Guy recited:

"In another life we were lovers.
You yearned for respect.
You yearned for affection.
I seldom listened."

"I'm sorry, Wade," I said.

"It wasn't your fault," whispered our tour guide. "Subconsciously you didn't want to feel the hurt you felt in your previous life. So, inside, you kept a safe distance from your mate."

"I forgive you," Wade replied.

My husband placed his arm around my shoulder. Guy stepped forward. The medieval scene vanished with the sunlight. Next, an enormous bed was lit by scarlet candles, as two lovers hid under the sheets, out of sight from our prying eyes. Words wrote themselves in classic calligraphy above their private space.

In another life we were royalty.
Our world was our own.
I held you tight.
We kissed, we slept.

"Money changes everything," I said.

"It always does," Wade replied.

"And here, without the concern of being paupers, I must have found the courage to give myself to my soul mate. All of me for our entire lives."

"Courage is a strange word to use. You found the comfort, Adam, not the courage."

"No, Wade, Adam is right," Guy replied. "There's a pattern here, and your husband has picked up on it, I think."

"Yeah, it takes courage to move on from the fear of losing your partner. Being royalty gave us the freedom to just be."

"I don't buy that," said Wade. "We were in a castle the life before this one. We were royalty of some sort. Adam, you should have gotten over losing me in that life."

"That's why some events are repeated, Wade," Guy explained. "In the medieval version, Adam, or Arthur, was busy protecting your lives. There were many enemies. So he kept you at a distance in case he lost you again." He gestured to the hidden lovemakers. "But here the universe got it right. You had a privileged life, so you began your relationship on the right foot."

"All very cosmic," my husband retorted. "But I see your point."

The scene faded to black. I felt the need to recite again.

"In another life we had a child.
Sand-castle building,
Insect collecting.

We had a child."

"I'm looking forward to this one," Wade said.

The sea calmly splashed toward us. I was barefoot, standing on golden sand. I tried to take it all in as the ripples blinded me with reflected daylight.

"William, keep an eye on our petal," I heard myself say in a woman's voice. "I need to swim."

I ran into the water, feeling my strange body jiggle in ways that as a man, I wasn't used to. Confused, I halted and gazed back.

"What is it, August?"

A beautiful man stared at me as his little girl rubbed sand into her golden locks.

"Look, Mummy, I'm washing my hair."

She shook her head, flicking small chunks from her scalp into William's face. He spat them out while laughing at his daughter's playful antics. Then he picked her up and ran toward me. And all the while, their neck-to-knee bathing suits didn't seem odd. In fact, they were kind of cute. Soon they were by my side.

"Why are you looking at our daughter like that?" William asked. He washed the sand from her hair.

"I know her," I replied.

"Of course you do."

"No. I mean I know her from elsewhere."

"Indeed you do," Guy interrupted.

We were back in our own bodies. Wade still had his arm around me as we stood in the darkness.

"She's Maude, isn't she?" I asked.

"Not yet. She's Maudi, star of the London stage when she grows up. Your love of the theater inspires her."

Guy sat on the edge of the pointed moon and encouraged us to do the same. We did.

"But Adam's right, isn't he? She's Maude as well."

The angel nodded.

"But how?"

"You have a cast of soul mates who weave in and out of your various lives. In the life you just saw, you encouraged Maudi to take to the stage.

And as Maude she has returned the favor."

"This is deep," I said.

"Yeah, like doing-my-head-in deep," Wade said.

"But sometimes you mortals repel the souls who arrive to teach you lessons, but they return when you're stronger and ready to learn."

Guy recited again:

"In another life we missed the boat.
We shared our lives,
Held back on love,
Then finally sailed."

Behind us, two young men dressed in black appeared. We stepped off our platform and onto an expanded floor that wasn't there a moment ago.

One of the men had dark skin like Wade and the other with light skin, like me. They bowed. We encouraged them with brief applause. They stepped closer together and fell into character.

"It's kind of cozy in here, Allan," said the elegant dark one.

"Warwick, spending the afternoon trapped in an elevator doesn't sound like fun."

He pretended to push buttons before yelling for assistance.

"It's not helping us."

"Well, you're not exactly coming up with answers. Why are you looking at me like that? Stop it. We have to get out of here and take the stairs."

The man playing Warwick kissed the forehead of the actor playing Allan, before his lips made their way to the man's neck. Wade and I shared guilty glances, yet I wasn't sure why.

"You don't know how long I've been waiting for you to do that," said the Allan character.

"I've had some idea. I've seen you give me that look."

"What look?"

He demonstrated.

"Really, is that what I look like? That's more post-orgasm than pre-orgasm."

"Then maybe actions speak louder than looks," replied the actor playing Warwick.

They kissed passionately, then broke away and bowed once more. We applauded again. They blew kisses at us and exited the stage.

"So we continued exploring our love," I said. "But that time as homosexuals."

"And we sailed, according to the poem," Wade noted.

"And we had Australian accents if the actors were accurate. And Allan was a white fella and Warwick was a black fella. Just like we are now. So why are we alike in nationality and race this time around?"

"Because your life ended too soon as Allan and Warwick," Guy replied.

"But we sailed according to the poem," my husband said again.

"Yes, you did, the last time you were here with me after you died." My angel peered down at his shoes. "Which is why I owe you both an apology."

"I can't imagine you ever owing me an apology, Guy," I replied.

"Let him speak, Adam."

He looked to us as the stars littered the sky again. The gentle light gave his face youth. No wrinkles on his forehead, yet there was a smidge of uncertainty in his smile.

"Adam, the two actors played you both in an unfinished life. Soon after, you and I became good friends. Which is why in the life you just lived I kept visiting you."

"There's nothing wrong..."

"Let me finish, Adam. It's against the rules around here. The mortal world is the mortal world, and this world is this world. I should never have introduced you to it before you died."

"Well, it didn't do any harm."

"Yes, it did. Just as I pined for you when you were reborn, you pined for me after I sorted out your midlife crisis."

"No, I didn't."

"Oh yes, you did," Wade replied. "The problem is, you don't remember."

"Which is why I'm saying sorry to both of you. My actions took Adam away from you, Wade. My need to reconnect with the first real friend I ever had tilted the balance of your final destiny."

"Wade, what's wrong?"

"Nothing, really. Just examining my own feelings."

"And what do they tell you, my husband?"

"I'm not sure. Adam, you prepared for all this even before you left me three years ago. This is all new to me, and a lot to take in. I hear your apologies, but how do I process this? A merry-go-round of past lives leading to what? To heartbreak and disloyalty. And sorry to say this, Guy, you're an angel who should've known better."

"Wade!" I was trying to reprimand him.

"No, Adam. Let him speak."

"I love you. I always have. But you're responsible for your choices, Adam. Guy may have interfered, but you didn't need to find other men."

"But Wade, there's more to this," Guy insisted. "Your husband needed you to believe in me."

"That's true, my darling," I said. "You argued that Guy was just a figment of my imagination. A figment that you and Maude thought helped me deal with Mannix's death. And look! Here's my guardian angel in front of your eyes. He's real! As real as you or me."

"That's not the point," Wade cried. "I was wrong for not believing you met your guardian angel. I admit it. But how does that excuse you from sleeping around and finding nirvana in strange places."

"Wade, there's something—" Guy tried to interrupt.

"Let me finish. I don't mean to blame you, Adam. Really, I don't. But see it through my eyes. Sure, I didn't believe you about your guardian angel. So what? Your actions after my disbelief should not have sent you away from me, both in life and in death."

"What can I say?" I mumbled.

My husband faced my angel. "I have a favor to ask. Can Adam stay with you tonight?"

"Of course." Guy sounded as timid as I felt.

"Just for tonight, my darling?" I asked.

He didn't answer. My guardian dispensed with the theatrics of flying us back home. One flash of light and I was with him in his apartment. Wade was obviously in ours.

Chapter Twenty

THE FOLLOWING DAY, Guy, Wade, and I stood near a cliff face. A few others could be seen sitting in the distance, as if they'd been there for a while. Over the edge, the blue-gray rocks crept down to meet the shadowy trees beneath. A river laid a path like an aimless snake finding its way through the dark forest.

"The problem is you don't trust me," echoed a male voice from below.

"The problem is you've given me no reason to trust you," replied a female.

I shivered. "That sounded like my mum and dad."

"It was," Guy replied. His voice had been gravelly all day.

The night before, I'd gone to bed early, but he had stayed up with a bottle of sherry nearby. Yet he had been functioning when I rose, even with his droopy wings and seedy face. I guess I underestimated the toll the previous day had on him.

"Where is this place?" Wade asked. "I mean, you keep doing that flash of light thing, Guy, and suddenly we're where we need to be. So where are we?"

"At the edge of the place we all live," he replied.

"And why is Adam hearing the voices of his parents?"

"Because this is the Valley of Lost Loves. You can listen to the conversations of lovers who never stayed together."

"That's kind of creepy," I said. "Why are we here?"

"I want you and Wade to walk in any direction and just sit and listen. I will stay here. I have my own listening to do."

I reached for Wade's hand, but he didn't notice. He strolled away while I quickly caught up. I looked back to my guardian, but he was already eavesdropping to other voices that rebounded from this lonely place.

"The Afterlife is getting weirder and weirder," my husband said.

"I'm more used to it than you are," I replied.

"Where are you going?"

"What do you mean? I'm going with you to listen in on other people's conversations."

"Adam, that wasn't me who asked that question."

"Well, it sounded like you, just with a little reverb."

We gazed into the valley.

"Adam, don't ignore me! Where are you going?" Wade's voice was questioning me from somewhere below. "I hate it when you don't talk to me."

I shuddered. "I remember that argument."

"You broke my heart that day," Wade replied.

"Why? We argued many times before."

"This was the point at which I knew there was no return."

His hand reached for mine. I held it. We eased ourselves onto the ground, sitting like the accused about to hear their verdict.

"Adam, I'm talking to you. Why are you ignoring me?"

"Why should I reply? You don't believe anything I say."

"If you are talking about bloody Guy again, I swear this marriage is over."

"Well, don't fret. I'm not running off to the Afterlife to see my guardian angel. How can I? He doesn't exist."

"Can I have that in writing?"

Wade turned to me. "Forgive me for not believing you, Adam."

"When something is so real in my life, it's natural to want to share it with my true love. So I did. You can't blame me for that. Besides, you know he's real now."

"Now I do, of course. But from the mortal world, how could I?"

"If you shut that door, Adam, don't bother coming back."

"More and more that doesn't sound like a threat, Wade."

The sound of a slamming door shot back at us like an exclamation mark. My husband chuckled. "One thing I can say about us is that we communicate."

"That's not what I expected you to say."

"Adam, there's something funny about hearing what we sound like when we argue."

I raised a brow.

"Where have you been?" Wade's voice echoed.

"Just one of those meetings again."

"Still trying to find your guardian angel, are you?"

"He's there somewhere."

I stared straight ahead.

"I knew you were playing around, Adam."

I gasped in guilt.

"I think a lover always knows, but if he doesn't admit it to himself, then he doesn't make it real."

"I can't even begin to tell you how sorry I am."

"No need to. You already have."

"You know, I still don't remember my amorous life, Wade."

My husband had the look of a priest contemplating the Lord. Noble and understanding, even when common sense told him otherwise. I doubted myself even more.

"Another meeting, Adam?"

"Another meeting, Wade."

"I remember that brief conversation," he said. "We hardly said much to each other at that stage. When I stopped raising my voice every time you left me, that's the point I stopped fighting for what I loved."

I gulped. "I remember that day well. You let me walk out the door without any sense of regret. But boy, did I feel regret. I drove down the street and sat in my car for an hour, just thinking."

"Yes, you came back early that night."

"You knew? You were asleep when I came home."

"I pretended to be asleep."

"I really wanted to talk when I came home."

"I wasn't sure if *I* did." I kissed his cheek, but there was no response.

"Maybe we should go back to Guy. I think he needs us. Besides, we've heard enough."

"I think you have a screw loose, Adam."

"Really, Wade, I'm not going crazy. Guy is real. Just take me at face value for once. Why would I carry on about an angel over and over again?"

"Like I said, you have a screw loose!"

"I really hated you that day," I said. "Yet for some reason, you raised your voice again."

"In hindsight, I can see why." He kissed me on the cheek. "That was the day, wasn't it? Maybe I sensed I'd never see you again."

"I went to that meeting because I really wanted to reconnect with Guy. After all, I already lost you."

"And I lost you that night in more ways than one."

His eye color had faded, like that of an old man who had seen too much sorrow. He allowed me to cradle his head on my chest, but he sat up as we heard the sobbing of a man and a woman.

"I'm hearing bells, August," said the male. His hoarse voice had an intonation like Wade's. "They're ringing for me, my love. Don't be sad. They're ringing for me."

"And if I could halt them, I would. I'm not going to lose you, Weldon. Listen to me and not the bells."

"They're calling for me, August. The angels are whispering my name. I will be forever your love, no matter where they take me."

"It's your fever that's whispering to you. You must block the voices out of your head for they are demons. They are demons who have come for you. Stay with me, Weldon, stay with me. For without you, I don't know how I'll survive."

The sound of the wind came from the valley, and in its whistle was the faint murmur of Weldon's name. August sobbed like an abandoned baby. Her cries shrill in our ears before sudden silence.

I was shaking like a leaf.

"Well, that was overly dramatic," Wade joked.

"I felt August's pain, and I began to really worry that I was losing you." I gasped with a shuddered breath.

"Are you about to cry, Adam?"

"I'm too shell-shocked to cry. As I listened, I had déjà vu. I knew every word August was about to say. As old-world as her language was, I could recite it like a play. Wade, I put you through hell, not only before I died, but for a good time after."

"It's okay."

"No, it's not okay. I was a real jerk, almost losing the person dearest to me. And what if I had lost you? I'd be screaming out your name, knowing I was the idiot who threw away nearly two decades of love."

"Hmm."

"What? That's all you have to say?"

"For the moment, Adam, yes, that's all I need to say."

"No, seriously, I was running away when I had everything I needed at home."

"Keep talking. I'm not stopping you."

"You're enjoying this, aren't you?"

"Uh-huh."

I stood, out of frustration more than anything else. Wade gave me a whimsical smile. I turned from him, but as I did, I saw Guy standing. His body hunched a little.

"Is he okay?" I asked.

"Adam, he's hungover."

"No. It's more than that. This whole experience is distressing him as well."

"Whatever Guy is feeling, perhaps he needs to feel it alone."

"No, I'm his friend. I need to talk to him."

"Seriously, Adam. He doesn't look like he wants company."

But my guardian spread his wings as he glanced at us. I waved. He strolled over, and from here, we wandered through the Art Deco Sector to make it home. I didn't say much as we walked. My sins kept playing over in my mind as Guy and Wade conversed about many things.

And I didn't stay with Wade that night. But that was my choice. I couldn't bear to lie next to a man I had taken for granted.

Chapter Twenty-One

GUY OFFERED ME a joint. I didn't accept it. It leisurely traveled to his lips as I tried to talk him out of it. I succeeded. He placed it on the coffee table.

"Seriously, I hardly slept last night," I said. "And dope for breakfast is not a good call." I took his hand. "I'm really worried about you. You love your substances too much. Why?"

"Adam, I'm supposed to be consoling you. Why don't we go for a drink?"

"Guy!" I stood and headed for his kitchen. "Orange juice will do."

As I poured, three sharp knocks came from the front door. I grinned to myself, hoping it was Wade. I grabbed a third glass.

"Are you ready to speak to me?" asked the voice at the door.

"Come in."

Josh meandered into the lounge room like a child whose best friend had moved out of town. Guy followed close behind with a perfect bunch of blood-red roses in one hand and a bag of marijuana in the other. I sighed to myself. The demon, in his angel disguise, caught sight of me in the kitchen as he positioned himself in front of the sofa. Guy subtly tilted his head toward the front door, signaling for me to leave.

"No, it's okay," said Josh. "I'm comfortable with Adam being here. I've got no secrets."

"Another bag of weed?" I called, still pouring orange juice. "You realize you're the reason he's a nervous wreck. A demon shouldn't have that much control over an angel."

"And I thought we were finally connecting, Adam."

"I'm starting to think you're a bit of a cad."

"Oh, how nineteenth century of you."

"No smartass comments, Josh. I'm sticking up for Guy."

"Adam, please," pleaded my guardian.

"It's okay, my love," the demon grumbled as he gave me a sly smile. "Power shifts when you know you're needed. Doesn't it, Adam?"

"What do you mean?" Guy asked. His wings fluttered twice. "What secrets are you two keeping from me? Has it anything to do with why Adam was in the Underworld?"

I snuck out of the kitchen feeling guilty and carefully placed the glasses of juice on the table.

"Now there's a suspicious walk. Hmm. Well, I guess if you two are bonding, I shouldn't see that as a negative."

Guy pursed his lips as we sat. At the same time, Josh shifted out of his angel disguise.

"Can I start this conversation?" I asked.

The wayward lovers nodded hesitantly.

"At the moment, I'm the last person to give advice on romance..."

They nodded vigorously.

"Hey! But I do have advice."

Now they stared blankly at each other.

"Just listen and pay attention. I want to start by reminding both of you how you felt when you first met."

Suddenly the discarded joint was in Guy's mouth. One breath in and it lit itself.

"Really, Adam?" the demon muttered. "Once again, I'm screwing up my love life, and you want to hear some romantic—"

Guy blew smoke into the demon's face, like a femme fatale seducing a detective.

"Joshua, you can't begin to realize how I felt when I met up with you again," the angel said in a soft tone. "I'll never forget all those years ago when you tried to teach me to fly. You were the confident one. Fearless. Nothing ever flustered you. Then there was me. Two left wings. No one but you to teach me to soar. I just didn't get the 'flight' thing back then. Soon you weren't around to teach me anymore. I felt I failed you and that's why you started keeping your distance. It was then I realized I had a crush on you.

"I finally found you again. My lost love. My hero. That guy I looked up to when I didn't have my parents around. But this time, I wasn't looking up to you. I was your equal. I could fly. I had responsibilities. I had people close to me that made me feel I was worth something. But your secrecy about my parents is not making me feel that I am worth anything."

"Guy, when I first met you, I was intrigued." Joshua's voice was lower than his boyfriend's. "Yes, you had two left wings, but you were interested in me. Up until that point, no one had been. Well, not in the way you were. Then I became captivated by you until that time I tried to teach you to fly." He paused. "Now hear me out. Yes, I left you as a teenager because I thought you were a loser. You were an angel and I thought flying would be the easiest thing to teach you. So I left, only to realize weeks later that I was missing you. I couldn't deal with feeling something for someone, so I ignored those feelings. In time, I forgot those feelings. But then I found you again."

"Hold on," I said. "First off, this is a conversation you should've had before now. In fact, it's one of those conversations you have right after the first time you have sex. Oh, that's right. You haven't had sex yet. Anyway, Guy, let me cut to the chase, because not knowing is making you into a drunken dopehead, even if you've mastered it with the elegance of an actress waiting on set. Now the reason why Josh hasn't told you where your parents are is because—"

There was another knock on the door. Josh rushed to answer it. Guy groaned before taking a second sophisticated puff.

"So, Adam. Where are my parents?"

"Guy, I should wait until..."

At the door were Mannix and Wade. I stood, almost knocking my juice from the table with my knee.

"Adam, if you don't close your jaw, you'll swallow a fly," said the angel.

"You're the boyfriend?" Wade asked Josh.

"The one and only," he replied.

They shook hands before Wade addressed me directly. "Before you say anything, Adam—"

"Yes," Joshua interrupted, "he does like to have the first word."

The two visitors strode past the door bitch.

"Damage control?" I asked Mannix.

"Damage control," he replied.

I mouthed the words "Thank you."

"He's given me the ins and outs of this place," Wade continued. "And yes, he's been in 'damage control.' He called me a hypocrite for blaming you for sleeping around after reminding me I fell into bed with him first."

"See, Guy," the demon announced. "We have nothing like the soap opera these two have. Our problems are child's play." He took the joint from the angel. "Oh, Adam, stop gawking at me like that. Your eyes will pop out."

"Pity, Josh. I was hoping you'd turn to stone."

"You need this smoke more than I do, pet."

I shivered as if ridding myself of bad karma. "So, Wade, is everything okay again?"

"Let's talk privately, Adam."

Mannix gave me a discreet nod.

"We could go back to our apartment. It's pretty crowded here."

"No. Guy's guest bedroom is fine."

My heart sank like it was wearing cement shoes. He led the way. I sat on the edge of my unmade bed.

Wade stood next to the window where outside the stark trees created a spooky setting for what looked to be a mime teacher with two students. With inner stillness, the instructor slid his hand down his smiling face as if putting on a mask. As his hand reached his chin, he revealed a frown. The eager learners did the same.

"I thought Joshua would be more, I don't know, demonic," my husband mused. "He's definitely as proud as you said he was."

"You've met him on one of his humble days."

"I see."

The mime tutor grabbed a piece of air and brought it to his heart. His pupils raised their hands as if releasing doves.

"I'm lost without your lips," I whispered.

"I know what that feels like."

"Then why are we estranged?"

"Adam, I'm not sure what I want to say, so just let me speak."

I tried to smile.

"I sold off every item of furniture, little by little after you died, to try to forget you."

"Yes, and I saw what you replaced it with."

Wade furrowed a brow.

"Okay, I'll keep quiet."

"Like I said, I sold every item of furniture to try to forget you, but I couldn't sell the sofa. It had our molded dents from watching too much television in it."

"At least we never got into reality TV."

"Yeah, but we watched too much of the box during winter, even if it was nice to snuggle on that sofa."

"We were at an age when blankets became our best friends." I grinned, noticing that outside, the mimes sat in a row with their legs crossed while drinking imaginary cups of tea.

"Adam, I realized we were an older couple when the things that used to annoy me about you became the things I missed most after you'd passed on."

"But that's just it, Wade. Relationships are about compromise, not sacrifice."

"That's not where I was leading with my last statement, but yes, we learned to compromise to the point where it didn't matter anymore."

The mimes now walked in an endless circle.

"There was nothing more to compromise, my husband. We were old enough to know where each other's minds were at. We had all our major arguments early in our relationship."

The mimes halted.

"Adam, I'm sorry I didn't believe Guy was real but put yourself in my shoes."

"I get it, Wade, I do. And because you didn't believe me, I drifted away. I had to, to find myself."

The performers now weaved aimlessly around each other, waving their arms in all directions.

"And I know you don't remember all those men you met, so it's like I have my old Adam back before you drifted off looking for love. But I need time to accept that you *are* my old Adam, not the drifter."

He moved forward so I puckered my lips. But he kissed me on the forehead.

"So I guess I'm staying in *this* room." I displayed a theatrical frown.

"Just give me time."

He wandered out. I didn't follow. Instead I watched the outdoor class again. They were all searching for something with their hands melodramatically placed above their eyes.

As they kept meandering, I focused on my small glimmer of hope. I knew my husband had to work through this. But surely after meeting Guy, he had to know I wasn't a fruitcake!

But infidelity is infidelity. Jealousy is jealousy. Loss is loss. I had my doubts about a happy ending. Our poem was off track. We had loved and lost so often in past lives, who was to say that in the Afterlife, other distractions wouldn't come into play?

"You should ask the Fifth Dimension for help."

Who said that? There was no one else in the bedroom with me. Outside, the mimes were all meditating. *Fifth Dimension?* That oddly rang a bell. I went back to the lounge room.

"Ever considered yourself as John Travolta?" Mannix asked Wade.

"*Saturday Night Fever* or *Pulp Fiction*?"

"Neither. Think *Hairspray*."

"Now guys, this is dangerous," said my angel, surprisingly coherent. "I can find another way to get to my parents."

"You told him?" I asked Josh.

"I didn't need to." The demon pointed at Mannix. "Your friend spilled the beans."

"Well, Guy hasn't been around much at the Guest Welcome Center," our young friend replied. "I want this rescue-his-parents deal over and done with so things can get back to normal."

"Rescue his parents?" I uttered. "More like a shady deal."

"I'm in!" my husband announced.

I wanted to grin but hid it.

"Um, so, *Hairspray*? I guess that means I'm doing drag."

"That's right," Mannix replied. "And Adam's directing." He turned to Guy. "With Adam directing, we're sure to get your parents out of that boring place."

"So, what play are we putting on?" I asked.

"I think we should do the play you cast me in when we first met. *Midsummer Mayhem*! Wade can be the society woman. I can be the boy toy again. Joshua and Guy can be in it as well!"

"Where are we going to find a copy of the script?"

With one snap of his fingers, Guy handed me a copy of this play, perfectly bound like it was a commercial release.

"I can't act," said Josh.

"But that's the point," Mannix replied. "Wade's in drag, and one of *you* will be as well. We'll send it up. That's sure to entertain the terminally bored."

"I have to do some negotiating with Preston while the play's on. You'll have to find someone else."

"But we need four actors," I explained. "Wade's playing Angela, a middle-aged woman with desires. Mannix is the object of that desire, her neighbor, Ronny. Now there's just Cecil, her husband, and Mary, the neighbor's wife. It's a four-hander. I need four actors."

"I could ask David," said Mannix.

"I don't think you should involve anyone else outside of us four," Guy warned. "I don't want to risk any other souls to the Underworld for my parents' rescue mission."

"I'll play the fourth character."

There was that voice again. The one that muttered something about the "Fifth Dimension."

"As a last resort, I might," Joshua said.

"No, seriously. I'm happy to play the role. No sweat."

There was no new person in the room, but Guy quickly made eye contact with me and just as quickly looked away.

"Come on, Joshua," Mannix begged. "For your boyfriend's sake."

"I don't know why you're even having this debate, Adam. You know you want me to play a role." The angel's wings fluttered once while I sat, thinking I could find sanity by easing deeper into the sofa. "Guy, tell Adam I want to be in his play."

Chapter Twenty-Two

Needless to say, I couldn't sleep again. Madness had come and found me. Voices would soon be telling me I was Jesus. At least at Guy's place, there'd be plenty of wine on hand.

Eventually, I stopped tossing and turning and sat up. For some reason, there was a toy rabbit in my dark room. I'd never noticed it before. I squinted to focus on the misplaced figure. Yes, it definitely was a rabbit.

"Steve, you have to concentrate on the bunny. Especially its eyes!"

That voice again? Lunacy was now my friend.

"I'd feel better with a dragon. They have mystical powers, you know."

A second voice? I closed my eyes to drown them out.

"But little cottontail here is the key to the Fifth Dimension."

"Mr. Trevor Murphy, why would a bunny be so mystic?"

Trevor Murphy? He was the lover I was supposedly with the night I was murdered! My eyes flicked open.

"Remember *Alice In Wonderland*? Remember *Donnie Darko*? Trust me! Bunnies are mystical."

The man, who had been the mime teacher outside Guy's bedroom window earlier that day, poised himself above the rabbit. Somehow the floppy toy was now seated on a dining chair.

"I'm still not convinced."

The other voice was now next to me in the shape of a man. A man not more than thirty with a smile that could charm the pants off a virgin. And should I mention his eyes? The color of milk chocolate, but with exotic eyelashes that drew you in with androgynous appeal.

"Adam, *you* understand the bunny gateway," Trevor pleaded. "Explain it to Steve."

"Well, only a bunny can take us to the Fifth Dimension." The words rushed out of my mouth like sewerage. "It's true that a dragon is mystical, but it only recognizes the third dimension. The elephant, poor thing, only takes us to first. And really, who wants to go there. The smell alone will get to you."

Steve's magic eyes studied me like I was his personal guru. *What a position to be in!*

"But the bunny has wisdom far beyond us mere mortals. It feeds us with its knowledge. But we have to decipher that knowledge carefully."

Where did that shite come from? Other males had come to light, seated around me at a dining table. Steve was repeating my words to himself as the others chatted quietly among themselves.

Trevor was still upright next to the stuffed animal, getting us to focus on its eyes while chanting something about a doorway to the Fifth Dimension. It seemed like an amusing way to dignify my insomnia, so I chanted.

Oh my god! The rabbit leaned forward.

"Adam, there are many ways to get back to the Afterlife," it said in a strange Russian accent.

I jolted, almost knocking my chair backward.

"Stop freaking out," Trevor said. "Each member of our order is getting their own message. Just run with it, Adam. You want to meet this guardian angel again, don't you?"

"Yes, you do, don't you, darling?" the creepy myxomatosis carrier asked—its voice highly pitched. "And you know just as much as I do, it takes a team effort to get you there."

"But if I just want to go back to the Afterlife, why do I need to open the Fifth Dimension?"

"Look into my eyes and see the answer."

"Riddles? Really! I get enough of those from Guy."

"Because the Fifth Dimension can take you anywhere," said Steve. "Even I know that."

The other men stared at me.

"Adam, you know the rules," Trevor asserted. "You communicate with the bunny through telepathy only."

"Sorry."

"Shall we start again?" asked a dreamy gent sporting classy metal-framed glasses.

"No," Trevor replied. "It's getting late. Time to organize our pairings for the night." He flicked his forearm like he was casting a fishing line as an elaborate way to simply point at me. "Adam, you're teaming up with Steve tonight."

"Yeah," said the young man. "I'm going to push buttons you didn't even know you had." He licked his lips. "Welcome to my lurve motel."

"Alfie, you're getting off with Andy and Andrew tonight."

"But I've already had Andy and Andrew," confessed the spectacled one. "Why don't we team up tonight, Trevor? You haven't seen my etchings yet."

"All right. Bill, do you want to take on Andy and Andrew this evening?"

"Yes," replied a bearded man with extra love handles. "I'm overdue for a threesome." He stood and walked to a middle-aged couple who looked like their mothers had cut their hair.

"That leaves Andre and Mack. You two haven't had sex yet, have you?" A dude hardly out of nappies and a rugged bloke in a worn leather jacket shook their heads. "Then it's game on."

The toy bunny leaned forward again.

"I think you've seen enough for today, sweetie." It blinked. *Its damn button eyes blinked!* "You're getting too much perspective too soon."

The scene faded, and there I was again, hunched on my bed. No freaky carrot muncher. No Fifth Dimension hopefuls. No sign of a dining room. But Trevor was still here.

"What?" I shrieked. "I don't get to have sex with Steve? He's hot!"

"Now, Adam. We can't live within the projections of the past." He smirked. "Did you want to have sex with Steve?"

"I recognize you," I said.

"I know. I can tell. But do you recognize the scene you just saw?"

"Yeah. Vaguely." I patted the spot next to me on the bed, so Trevor joined me. "Why did you pair us all up at the end?"

"So that we're one intense and open force. A combined force to help take us to the Fifth Dimension."

"And I slept with all those guys?"

"Let's just say, you were creative." He smiled with no hint of sleaze.

"Did I make it to this new dimension?"

"Yes, you did, Adam," said Guy's voice. His majestic wings materialized before the rest of him. "That is how you were able to visit Wade without my help."

"So that's how I did it. Did I use this dimension while I was alive?"

"You started to, but Trevor's ex stopped you both before your first astral travel."

"So what exactly is this Fifth Dimension?"

"I'm afraid it was just a fancy name we came up with for our group," replied my fellow murder victim. "We didn't know if we could tap into the power, but you and I did."

"That doesn't answer my question. What is the Fifth Dimension?"

"Trevor's told you," my angel replied. "It's a way a group of horny men got together, dabbled in a little astral traveling, and tried to solve their own mysteries."

"That's harsh, Guy," Trevor said. "We were more than that."

My guardian's neck swiveled deliberately as his deadpan expression took aim at my former friend with benefits.

"Now listen. If you didn't invite Adam to your exclusive sex club, he and Wade would still be alive and happy."

"And if you didn't show yourself repeatedly to him during his lifetime, he'd never have tried to seek you out after your last good-bye."

"He's got a point, Guy," I said. "I missed you. Wade didn't believe I had seen you, so I guess I was looking for two things that I missed. One was intimacy, the other, your friendship. Even *you've* acknowledged my motives in your apology to me."

Trevor mimicked my angel's gradual neck move earlier, except a cheeky grin was what he shared. Guy smirked back, then sat with us.

"So you want to be in the play?" my winged companion asked. Trevor nodded. "We can't let Wade know your real name. He'll know who you are."

"I don't want you in my play," I said.

"Then I'll have to talk Joshua into being in the play."

"You know there's little chance of that," Trevor said. He paused momentarily. "I'll do the play. I'll change my name. And only you two will know who I am."

"But Wade will recognize you," I said.

"He won't," Guy replied. "He never met Trevor."

"But his face would have been on the news. On the internet. The shocking murder of Adam and his lover, Trevor!"

The angel shook his head.

"What are you saying?"

"Wade was in shock. He didn't want to know, so he kept to himself. No TV. No internet."

"So you *were* keeping an eye on us during my final days."

"Most of the time, Adam."

"Most of the time? What do you mean?"

"That's not important right now."

"Guy!" I crossed my arms.

"When this standoff is complete, I'd still like to put my hand up to be in the play," Trevor said. "And for Wade's sake, I'll change my name."

"Okay," I mumbled. "You should take on the character of Mary, the neighbor?"

"Thanks. I had my fingers crossed for the other drag role."

"Why don't you want me in drag?" Guy asked. "I'm a stunner in lipstick and a long blonde wig." He fluttered his eyelashes, breaking me out of my sulky mood.

"Because you don't strike me as a drag queen. No offense. But seriously, an angel in drag? I mean, I don't really see you in the role of Cecil, either. But you're more suited to Cecil than Mary." I bit my bottom lip. "Besides, can you imagine casting Trevor as Wade's spouse? My husband and my adultery partner would be an onstage couple. That's not a good idea."

"Oh, I don't know," my random lover replied. "You could watch us interact onstage and imagine yourself in the middle."

I slapped him playfully.

Chapter Twenty-Three

"So WHO IS he, Adam?"

Mannix was playing detective as we stopped for a break. We had just finished our initial script reading and the cast were munching Wade's homemade almond cookies. I tried to make myself a cup of tea, but my young friend kept interrupting me with his investigative tone.

"Like I already said, he's an actor friend of Guy's."

"You can't pull the wool over my eyes. I've seen the way he looks at you."

"Well, maybe he has a thing for me? I don't know. But I've never met him before in my life. Or in the Afterlife for that matter."

Mannix crunched his sugary treat while watching Trevor chat to Wade and Guy at the other end of the community hall. Guy, who was surprisingly sober, had organized this rehearsal space, which felt more like someone's weatherboard home than a public place. The kitchen felt homely with the odor of freshly lacquered carpentry from its newly installed cabinets. A wall coated with blackboard paint brought us new perspectives from the chalk musings of enthused children, who used this room for art class.

Of course, we had to change Trevor's name to something he suggested. Guy and I thought it was a silly name, but Trevor insisted. So we bit our tongues.

"I saw the way you two looked at each other when he came in. You two have a history. I know it!"

"I think your imagination is working overtime."

"I know unfinished business when I see it."

I observed the risky communication between my husband and my secret murdered companion.

"Mannix, seriously, I've never met Ziggy before today."

"Well, you're taking more than a director's interest in him. And he's taking more than an actor's interest in you."

"Nonsense."

I clapped my hands twice to attract everyone's attention. It was time to get back to rehearsal, and to stop Mannix's curiosity. Trevor raised his hand.

"Adam, about my character," he inquired. "I'm obviously older than Mannix, but Mary isn't. So as a couple, there'll be years between us. Should I stick with my own age, or try to look young?"

"Try to look young, Ziggy, because Mannix's character is tempted by your older neighbor. If you're just as old, then his attraction makes no sense." I pointed toward the kitchen. "I have a couple of wigs for you to try on. Wade, yours is the one with tight curls. Ziggy, the long blonde one obviously."

Trevor popped his on and checked himself in the small mirror near the sink. He brushed the hair from his eyes, then erected himself like a fashion model. Elegant fingers pointed outward as he stepped daintily past the sandwiches I'd prepared for lunch. He paused. He attempted to pick one up while pretending his nonexistent fingernails were in the way. Then he faced us and tried his best Vogue pose.

The team laughed, but I was taken with his form. As he peeled off the wig, his rosy lips and wild green eyes beckoned me with intense familiarity.

His tall grace, even in stillness, commanded a room like the perfect performer. Self-assured. Quiet. Hypnotic to watch.

He stretched upward, reminding me of his physique. Under that black T-shirt was a chest to blissfully nuzzle your face into. His legs, from memory, held most of his power within their sculptured mass. Strength to thrust and never give in. And yet these thoughts seemed unfounded. *What is going on in my head?*

"I like you, Ziggy," said Wade. "It's a shame Adam and I didn't know you when we were alive. You would have been a hit at the Petersham Theatrical Society. Don't you think, Adam?"

Guy had a look of horror.

"Um. Yeah!" I replied. "Yes, Wade, he would have been perfect for so many plays. Ziggy, why hadn't we met in theater circles?"

"Because I was running around acting in short film projects," he answered. "I avoided theater. Too much commitment."

My angel was smirking.

"It's a shame," Wade said. "But we're going to have fun acting together."

Trevor and Wade pulled on their wigs. They sashayed out of the kitchen and onto the stage where a table, four chairs, and dining implements awaited.

Wade, as Angela, sat next to Guy, who was playing his husband, Cecil. They took the middle chairs while Mannix, as Ronny, sat opposite his stage wife, Mary, played by Trevor, who was masquerading as Ziggy. I instructed them to use upper-class British accents.

"What do you mean you're leaving me?" Wade roared as Angela.

"I'm bored," Cecil replies.

"Who is she?"

"There's no one else."

Angela turns to their dinner guests. "What am I going to do for money?"

"Maybe you can marry Tony?" Trevor suggested as Mary. He wiggled sass from every pore.

"He's poor."

"But he's famous. It's only a matter of time before he makes some money out of it."

"What about Carter?" Mannix asked as Ronny. "He's loaded!"

"But look at his connections," Cecil snipes. "At least I'm leaving you instead of hiring a hit man to dispose of you."

"This simply will not do," Angela protests. "We can't split up if there's no one else involved. What will the papers say?"

"I know what to do," Mary jokes. "I'll have an affair with your husband."

"Splendid!" the hostess exclaims.

"And so will I," Ronny jests. "You'll get lots of sympathy."

"No, that's way too scandalous. Mary, you have the affair with my husband."

Mary chokes on her wine while clutching Ronny's hand.

"But there's still the question of money," Ronny says.

"I shall write a bestselling book," Angela replies.

"What about?" Cecil asks, rolling his eyes.

"About your affair and my years as a dear faithful wife. So you better have a spicy affair, Mary!"

"Where should they be caught?" Ronny asks. "In bed?"

"Ronny!" his wife shrieks.

"I picture the perfect setting," Cecil replies. "Dutch clogs, a house plant, and five pounds of strawberry ice cream.”

"Ah, the memories,” Angela declares wistfully.

"Why would they make love in the kitchen?” Ronny asks.

"Ronny!” his wife shrieks again.

"I wasn't picturing a kitchen,” Cecil replies. “I was picturing a barn.”

"Fully or partially naked?” Angela asks.

"Definitely fully.”

"You realize, Mary, you'll have to stay naked until the reporters arrive.”

Cecil winks at Mary as she turns to her husband in fear.

"Help!” Mary gasps.

"Thank you, Mary.” Angela pats her neighbor's hand. “You're such a dear friend.”

Ronny stands, about to take his wife out of this madhouse.

"April fool!” the hosts sing in unison.

"Bravo,” I applauded. “But how did you remember your lines so fast? We only read the script this morning.”

"Search me,” Wade replied. “That's never happened before.”

"Guy, is this some other trick in the Afterlife? We remember our lines instantly?”

His wings fluttered thrice. “Well, you have to admit it will speed things up.”

The day wore on productively. Words were spoken with intent. Subtle nuances crept into the body language of my players. And everyone's timing hit the mark on many wonderful lines.

This was a play that centered on Angela's seduction of Ronny. Knowing my husband and Mannix had history, I knew they could pull off the subtext with ease. The other characters would have to keep us entertained in the short scenes they were in.

Getting Wade to play it straight in drag, while getting Mannix to weave around his advances, would be my winning formula in getting the jaded Underworld crowd to enjoy themselves. I mean, if we played strictly for laughs, there was a good chance we'd come off as amateurs and fail to entertain.

Before the scenes where Angela's playful urges would try to get Ronny into bed, I had to direct Trevor and Wade together in a scene. I was freaking out a little. *What if I slip and forget to call him Ziggy? What if Wade picks up on who he is?* I blocked my fear and asked them to run through it.

My doe-eyed secret lover sat with my husband, drinking cranberry juice impersonating as red wine. Wade's motions were grand like a woman of the upper crust, while Trevor played ditzy with ease.

"At his vintage, I never believed for a minute Cecil was thinking of leaving you." Blonde-wigged Trevor places his hand on his cheek.

"Oh, you're too kind, Mary. But at his vintage, I'm surprised he's still alive." Wade patted the side of his spiral locks while he shook his head.

"You mustn't say that, Angela. He's still got a spring in his step."

"Yes, but these days, he's as useful as a sundial. Once the sun goes down, he does too."

"I don't believe it. Why, the fun you still have together. That's surely an indication of what's happening in the bedroom."

"Mary, stop worrying about the private life of your neighbors. There must be kinder topics of conversation." Wade sipped his juice. "Like your love life."

"My love life?"

"Yes. Ronny's a strapping young man. I'm sure he fulfills all *your* needs." Trevor displayed a devilish smirk.

"Well, Ronny is from the finest breeding. Athletic and educated, like most of his family."

"And are you enough for him?"

"Well, I hope I am." My secret lover stands, hand to bosom.

"No, dearie, I'm just saying. Sit down, please. Your stature is making me feel like a costar."

He eases down gradually. "Well, you are throwing accusations."

"Oh, Mary, Cecil has had lots of affairs. Do I cry? No. I'm a woman of empathy. I'm a woman of understanding. I'm a woman who's devoted."

"And his other infatuations aren't an issue?"

"Not at all."

"The smell of another's perfume?"

"Mere distraction."

"Lipstick on the collar?"

"A good presoak and the stain comes out. That's what the maid says."

"Various mouths in various places?"

"Dip him in bleach and the bacteria is gone!"

I shuddered. Art was imitating life. And one of my suitors was onstage with my husband.

"Was that okay?" Wade asked.

"Perfect," I uttered.

"You look like you're not happy with it. Do you want us to do it again?"

"No. No. No. It's fine."

"This really is a play about adultery, isn't it?" Trevor asked.

"On so many levels," Mannix replied. He and Guy sat on director's chairs behind me. "That's why I picked it. It's sure to win over the walking dead, let alone Preston's lot."

"Shall we..." I began.

"Shall we what?" Wade asked.

"Shall we move onto one of the, you know, one of the seduction scenes?"

"What is it, Adam? You seem distracted."

Trevor was pouting outside Wade's line of sight.

"I knew you two had history," Mannix whispered.

Guy's wings almost fluttered.

"Mannix, get onstage. Ziggy, you can come down now. Um. I might just make a cup of tea while you get in position."

But Wade stepped off stage and followed me into the kitchen.

"I'm so glad Guy found Ziggy," he said. "He's a really good actor, even in a wig."

"Err. Yeah. He is."

I accidentally put salt in my tea. I poured another.

"It's a shame neither of us met him while we were alive. He's a really nice guy."

"That he definitely is."

The milk was in the fridge door, but I couldn't see it.

"We should get to know him. I think he has lots of tales to tell." Wade handed me the milk.

"Thank you."

"Adam, do you think he had a boyfriend when he was alive?"

"Oh, a guy like that was probably beating them off with a stick."

"True. He's really sexy. He probably plowed most of his postcode."

I nearly choked on my first gulp. "He might be a busy man. He may not have time to hang around with us."

"Let's ask him." Wade led the charge as I followed timidly. "Ziggy, are you free for dinner tomorrow night? I'm cooking."

Chapter Twenty-Four

"HOW LONG HAVE you known Guy?" Wade asked.

My husband wasn't stingy with the red wine. Both my glass and Trevor's were filled to the brim. I shoved a plate of roast potatoes in our guest's face as he ignored my panicked expression.

"Guy and I go way back," he replied. "We initially met when I taught him yoga. We've been friends ever since that first lesson."

I rolled my eyes. "How does an angel do yoga? I mean, what do his wings do when he lies on his back?"

"They spread out."

He poked his tongue out at me as soon as Wade turned to head for the kitchen.

"Really, Ziggy? Think about it. Imagine bridge pose. Only the back of his head, his feet, and his arms are on the floor. Wouldn't his wings get scrunched up behind his elevated back?"

"He points them out and flutters them, keeping the other students cool with the air he circulates."

I stuck *my* tongue out this time. Wade returned with a succulent deboned chicken with several slices already cut. Butter and herbs oozed from the middle of this roasted delight. He spooned the enticing filling back over our dinner as the aroma intensified.

"Yum!" said Trevor and I in unison.

"You two have a connection," said Wade.

"Who? Us two?" I said. "You're imagining things, husband. Why, if it wasn't for Guy, I still wouldn't know who this person is. Would I, Ziggy?"

"But Wade has a point," he replied.

My eyes widened.

"I'm not saying you've met before," Wade continued. "It's just that for two people who haven't known each other that long, you act like old friends.”

“He’s right, Adam. You and I have a mystical connection.” He winked when my husband was placing chicken on my plate. “I know we’ve only known each other for a short time, but I feel I’ve known you longer.”

“Ziggy, I don’t think so,” I said through gritted teeth.

“No, Adam, listen to him,” Wade stressed. “You bounce off each other like high school friends.” He peeled the aluminum wrapping from the garlic bread and offered it to our guest. “Ziggy, did you know anyone from the Petersham Theatrical Society?”

“No, but after meeting both of you, I wish I had.”

“Did you ever go to art class?”

“No. I can’t even draw stick figures.”

“Did you know our friend, Maude?”

“I don’t know any Maudes.”

“Where else could you have met?”

A sense of guilt made me butt in. “Wade, if Ziggy and I had met each other before, don’t you think we would have remembered?”

“He’s got a point. Adam and I would remember meeting.”

“I suppose you’re both right,” my husband replied. He bit into a baked potato.

Kylie Auldist’s vocals swooned from the stereo with an infectious blues spirit. Her soulful voice gave me something to focus on as Trevor kept sharing discreet glances with me, which I tried to ignore.

“Now *this* is music,” he said with a mouthful of poultry.

“She’s a Melbourne lass from the early twenty-first century,” Wade replied. “She’s one of our favorite retro artists.”

“I had a feeling you had good taste.” He aimed his remark at me. “I love female singers that nourish the soul. I also like tragic singers that entertain us for all the wrong reasons. But when you hear a voice like that, you still know some part of you is alive.”

I nearly choked on a snow pea. “Wow, you’ve become a chicken-chomping guru,” I said. “But yesterday at rehearsal, you were the king of camp. Did you leave your swinging hips at our front door?”

“Darling, Adam. I never lose my camp. It’s just in my back pocket while we eat.”

“I think Ziggy and I will steal the show in the Underworld,” said Wade.

"We're the dames of this theatrical adventure. We'll have the audience laughing from the first scene."

"I sure as hell hope so," I confessed. "Guy is a close friend, and I don't want to let him down. So make sure you entertain the pants off those bored individuals. They need a laugh."

My husband patted my shoulder, then added a couple more potatoes to my plate.

"You know, your relationship is pretty cool." Trevor accentuated his point by pointing with his fork. "There's still a lot of mileage in your marriage."

I swallowed hard. Wade headed back to the kitchen.

"I forgot something," he called back to us.

I studied the table. "What did you forget?"

"Salt and pepper."

"But they're already on the table."

"Sour cream for the potatoes."

He returned with a bowl of the creamy substance. Neither of us touched it.

"During rehearsal, I couldn't help notice how in sync *you* both are," Trevor continued. "I mean, you think Adam and I are in sync. Yesterday, Adam gave you direction and you telepathically knew what he wanted before he finished his sentence."

"But my Wade is a top actor. Even if *I* wasn't directing, he'd have no issues following direction from anyone else."

"Adam, there's still a bright spark in both of you when you talk to each other."

"What? We could've saved on power bills back home just by talking to each other?"

My husband weighed in. "The way you talked through movies we watched, Adam, we could have unplugged the television and it would have still worked."

"See," our guest said. "You work off each other. A real couple does that. Adam and I just act like friends getting to know each other."

Wade looked at me like a stage singer who'd forgotten the words.

"Ziggy, where did you learn to act?" I asked.

His arms fanned out like water from a sprinkler. "Nowhere. I was born to perform."

"Yes. Especially in a wig and a dress. But really, where did you learn?"

"I've done a bit of drag, that's all."

"Well, you're a natural. Isn't he, Wade?"

"I really thought you went to drama school or something," my husband replied.

"Seems like it's a night of compliments."

His mouth was stained red from the wine. I looked at my wine as if it would give me an indication of the color of my own lips. Wade slopped a spoonful of sour cream on his half-eaten potato. And we chomped quietly as our dinner music filled the gap of our sudden lull in conversation.

We finally retired to the lounge, all a little more relaxed as the second bottle of wine was poured.

"Go on, I dare you." Trevor had a challenge for Wade.

"My husband is just being coy," I said.

"I'll find my courage after one more glass," Wade replied.

"Leave it to me." I headed for the second bedroom and pulled out a large plastic container. "Found it!"

My husband's eyes lit up as I dragged the box into the living room. "It's just like the one we had at home."

"What is it?" Trevor asked.

"It's a costume box," I replied.

"Did you both dress up before going to bed?"

Wade looked at me like a patient worried about his blood test. I gazed back, smiling hard. I needed him to lighten up, if just for tonight. After all, I wanted to move back in with him, but trust is a hard thing to win back. I opened the container.

"That's what I wore to Maude's medieval party!" Wade said. He pointed to the purple robe sitting on top of the costume pile. I pulled it out and draped it across my extended arm. "It's exactly the same."

"This place still does my head in," said Trevor. "I've been here for nearly a year and I still find things at my place that are exactly like what I had back in Sydney. Even the odd sex toy!"

"Adam, remember that party?"

"How could I forget?" I replied. I crouched next to the box, still with the robe on my arm, and found a ratty brown wig. "This was your costume. Maude said you looked like the town spinster who desperately needed a prince with a glass slipper."

"And you wore a pirate outfit, even though none of us knew how that tied in with the Middle Ages."

"It wasn't a pirate outfit." I found the getup and pulled it out of the container. "It's a jousting outfit. See, it's black with white around the edges. Pirate, indeed!"

Wade shook his head.

"Ziggy, you can see it's a jousting outfit, can't you?"

"I'm still eyeing off that tacky wig." Trevor grabbed it and rushed to the bathroom. "Do you have a hairbrush?"

"Ziggy, we're both bald. What would we need with a hairbrush?"

He returned, shoved it on his head, grabbed his wineglass, and sashayed around the room.

"Well, let me just say, gentlemen, that you are both the perfect hosts." His voice sounded like a strangled cat. He then took a drink, making sure to extend his pinkie. "And to think you called me up as soon as you heard I didn't have a date for tonight. You two are so thoughtful."

Wade stood and offered his hand. "Pardon me, Miss, but I've forgotten your name."

Trevor took it while fluttering his eyelashes. "That's totally understandable, my dear." He slipped into the accent of a Southern belle. "I go by many titles. Some call me the Hussy of Hound Dog Lane. Some think of me as the upstanding citizen as pure as a Christian saint. Others know me for my fund-raising work. But few know my name."

"That's because you're still trying to think of one, Ziggy," said Wade. He peered down his nose at our melodramatic guest.

"That's it. I'm Madame Ziggy! Starlight conceptual artist making cowboys think about their mortality..."

"What's a '*starlight* conceptual artist'?"

"I perform during starlight, so my complexion looks its best."

"If you're Madame Ziggy, doesn't the 'Madame' signify that you run a house of ill repute?"

"Darling, I've been known for many things, including my finesse at entertaining a gentleman caller."

"So how could a Madame be as pure as a Christian saint?"

"Oh, Wade, for goodness sake!" He dispensed with the accent. "Just find another wig and join me."

I fetched the hairpiece he'd wear in my play and slapped it on his head. "So what's your name?" I asked my husband.

"Wendy."

"Wendy?"

"What's wrong with Wendy?"

"Too wishy-washy."

"What about Wanda?"

"No. With a name like that, you'd have a tutu and a magic wand."

"Wilhelmina," suggested Trevor.

"Really? That has homely written all over it."

"I agree with Adam, Ziggy," my husband said. "I know! I'm Willow."

There was a knock at the door. "A hippy name suits you," I said as I went to see who was there. "I've seen you at your vaguest."

"What do you mean?"

"Wade, we've been together forever. I've seen every facet of your personality."

Mannix stood at the entrance. "What are you doing here, Adam?" he whispered. "Have you moved back in?"

"No. Wade and I are keeping up appearances for Ziggy."

He listened while having the expression of someone who'd just sipped sour milk.

"Is it a battle to see who has the more girlish voice?"

"Possibly. You'd swear they were old friends."

Now Mannix looked like he had failed an important exam.

"What's the matter?"

"What makes you think something's the matter?"

"There have been many times during our friendship I've seen that look on your face. Something's wrong. What is it?"

He bit his bottom lip.

"It's David, isn't it?"

"You've got a guest. I'll only bring down the mood. I'll take my problems to Guy."

"He's not home. I think he's gone out with Josh."

"Hopefully to communicate better."

"Who is it?" called my husband in a drag tone.

"It's Mannix."

Madame Ziggy and Willow flounced to the front door.

"Why, it's a gentleman caller," exclaimed the Southern belle. He'd wrapped my jousting costume around his waist to create a crude skirt. "I've heard about Señor Mannix. He's the playboy of the Deep South."

"Suddenly I'm Mexican?" our friend asked.

"Just go along with it," I replied.

"But in my circles, he shares the wisdom of the gods," said Wade. He had cocooned himself inside the purple robe, resembling a flower child the morning after a bad acid trip.

"Are they stoned?" Mannix asked.

"Just drunk," I replied.

Trevor took our guest by the arm and escorted him to the living room. Wade and I followed. I then made a beeline for the kitchen and grabbed another wineglass. Our Madame poured.

"Now tell me, Señor, what is a good-looking guy like you doing in a place like this?" Trevor dragged him onto the couch next to him. "Did you come to see me?" More fluttering eyelashes.

"Where's David?" Wade inquired.

I put my finger to my lips.

"Shouldn't I ask?"

"It's okay, Adam," our young friend replied. "We had a fight."

My husband took his wig off. Trevor followed his lead.

"What happened?" I asked.

"I guess I wasn't enough for him."

"He's found someone else?"

"He did."

"He *did*? So it's nothing permanent? It's just a one-night stand?"

"Yeah, but it still hurts." Mannix and Wade exchanged guilty glances before our heartbroken friend lowered his head. "Sorry for being a hypocrite, Adam."

"A hypocrite? You're far from that." I reached over and placed my hand on his knee.

"A hypocrite?" asked Trevor.

Wade giggled nervously for a moment before we met eyes.

"Should I go home and leave you to talk?"

"No, Ziggy," I answered. "It's quite okay. We're about to do a play together to rescue Guy's parents, so as a fellow actor, you should get to know our relationship."

"What Adam is trying to say is…" Wade paused and gazed at me like a gambler who just lost his life savings. "Um, er, you see, Ziggy, I may have instigated the demise of our marriage."

"No, you didn't, my charming husband."

"But you two were the perfect hosts tonight." He stopped. I could only deduce that he'd forgotten our cosmic swingers group momentarily. This secret alone was increasing its weight on me. "Adam and Wade, I meant what I said earlier. There's still a lot of mileage in your relationship." He stood, peeled off his makeshift skirt, and picked up his glass. "I know a lot of married gay men, and this is something I don't say lightly, but I still see a mountain of love between you guys. Don't take that for granted."

"Ziggy, I'm living with Guy at the moment."

"A bit of time out now and again is good for a relationship."

"Is it?"

"I slept with Mannix." My husband simply blurted it out.

"No! Really? You and him? Get out of here!"

"Yep, and what happened after that caused unending ripples." My husband sat.

"Now, Wade," I said, "having a threesome with Mannix isn't exactly what caused ripples. Perhaps what I got up to after…"

"Really? You and him *and* him? Get out of here!"

"Has everyone forgotten I'm in the room?" Mannix asked.

"And how did you instigate getting these old men to sleep with you?"

"Old men?" His eyes met ours back and forth, with the expression a champion sportsman gives to his coach in gratitude. "The thing you have to learn about Adam and Wade is that to each other, there is no one else. Well, that's not exactly true. Their friends come in a close second, collectively."

"Listen to him, guys." Trevor sat as he spoke. "Your image is being reflected back to you."

Mannix stood with his glass raised. "When you first meet Adam and Wade, you learn quickly that these two names are synonymous. One name doesn't roll off the tongue without the other name following instantly. Together they're a force to be reckoned with. The love and respect they show to a newcomer hits like a bolt of lightning, but soon you're lifted from your bewilderment by heart-to-heart communication, confidence building, and straight-out friendship."

Trevor rose and clinked glasses with Mannix. "You can't fake that kind of respect, men."

I blew Wade a kiss. He didn't respond.

"The only thing more important than their friendship to others," Mannix continued, "is the friendship they've built around each other. They work together in any situation, and I'm one of the privileged few to have experienced their marriage, warts and all." He was about to sip. "Yes, warts and all."

"That sounds like an epiphany," Trevor declared.

"Remember when you berated me, Adam?" Mannix asked. "I was diving for cover any way I could."

"What was he mad at you for?"

"Nothing, really," I said. "I was being silly."

"But I understand why you were mad," Mannix continued. "I had sex with Wade behind your back. And at this point in time, I really get how you felt."

He downed his wine and headed for the front door.

"Where are you going?" Wade asked.

"To find David."

"But aren't you angry at him?"

"How can I be? I was once just as reckless and stupid!"

Chapter Twenty-Five

THE SOUND OF Herb Alpert and the Tijuana Brass wafted about, as Guy, Mannix, Joshua, Trevor, Wade, and I wandered down the stairs to the Underworld.

"You're right, Adam," Wade whispered. "This place really is Hell."

"Wait till you meet the inhabitants. They actually like this type of music."

Preston greeted us. His trademark top hat and pearls were matched with a vivid red vinyl vest and tight pants.

"Hello, my thespian friends." His resonant voice hit me with its bass. "You must be Wade, and you must be Ziggy, our dames of the theater. I have the perfect outfits for you. I see you've brought your own wigs."

"My long blonde look has become part of me," Trevor declared.

"Spoken like a true method actor," Wade replied.

I cringed. I was buying time before Trevor's past relationship to me would be discovered. How the secret wasn't revealed over dinner is anyone's guess. And here they both were, my husband and my last living lover as best friends, while I still lived with my guardian angel.

"I hope things are better in your relationship than they are with mine," I whispered to Mannix.

"They couldn't be better. I mean, new relationship, he slipped, no big deal." He smirked.

"Makeup sex?"

"Makeup sex!"

"I'm glad I finally got to meet the other players," said Preston. "Including you, Guy. This is an important night for you."

The angel forced a smile.

"I'm surprised you're in the cast—" Preston continued.

Josh waved his hand vigorously behind his boyfriend's back.

"—But I guess you have your reasons."

I looked at Josh, but he shook his head when I made eye contact. When we made our way past the entrance and into the harem, Wade and Trevor stopped to admire the scenery.

"They're all so young," Trevor noted. "I don't know whether to make love to them or adopt them."

A gravelly voice sang to a blues guitar, which drowned Herb Alpert's muzak from the other room. The tune spun from a turntable as the caged boys gyrated like desperate go-go dancers.

"At least the music and the décor are better in this room," Wade said.

Trevor patted him on the shoulder. "Can we invite them into the audience?" he inquired. "Or better still, onstage? I'm sure we can make use of them."

"They can be Angela's hired help. And that one over there would make the perfect pool cleaner."

"Enough already," I said.

"They have their own special job to do," Preston replied. "And it ain't cleaning house." He waved his hand above his hat. "Follow me, everyone. An audience awaits."

As we went through the next door, I noticed a buzz in the air. The varied forlorn faces from my previous stay seemed more upbeat. There was chatter, movement, and a few smiles.

"They look like clones in those drab clothes," Wade noted quietly.

"Well, at least you won't be upstaged by the audience," I replied.

We wandered through each room, including the Parking Museum, until we got to Preston's hidden wardrobe.

"Now this is what I call a costume department!" Trevor declared.

He ran into the open space, touching almost every garment he passed. Wade followed close behind. Preston picked up a lime dress with a stained apron sewed onto it.

"This is for the Angela character. Which one of you is playing her?"

My husband stared in horror at the outfit, then at me.

"No," I shrieked. "That's the wrong look for Angela."

"I don't care. It's the look I want her to have. It will be hilarious!"

"Preston, the idea is to play it straight. It makes it funnier with Wade in drag. If we play for laughs, we'll fail. Besides, Angela doesn't do her own housework."

"Adam, darling, trust me. I have a theatrical bent. I know the crowd you're working with. This will have them rolling in the aisles." He held up another dress. A cosmic sixties number with more colors than a box of crayons. "And this is for Mary."

"But she's a plain Jane."

"Not in my production, she's not."

"It's *my* production, Preston."

"It's my venue, Adam. Just think of me as the producer, giving life to you all so you can do what you do best."

He showed off another psychedelic outfit for Mannix's character, Ronny. Again, totally wrong. And Guy was given a grandpa cardigan. There was no hint of upper crust for my Angela and Cecil.

"Should you be interfering with the director's vision?" I asked.

"Adam has a point, Preston." It was Josh speaking up for me. "He's worked hard directing this play for a chance to free Guy's parents. And you're crippling their chances."

"I don't see it that way. I see it as providing inspiration to a cast directed by a man who takes life too seriously. Lighten up. My changes will work. It's called slapstick."

"Wow!" Trevor exclaimed. We all glanced his way. "Look at this wig." He fondled a blonde extravaganza that was large enough to anchor a ship. "I have to wear this."

"The theater was invented by the queeniest of cavemen," Preston proclaimed. He took the wig off its stand and plopped it on the actor's head. "It's all yours, Ziggy." Then our host rubbed his hands together like a clichéd villain. "I'll leave you theater folk to it. Joshua and I have some things to discuss. When you're dressed, just come out to the main conference area. That's where you'll be performing." They toddled off together.

"Should we try to get the apron off my outfit?" Wade asked.

"What do you think those stains are?" Mannix mused.

"Nothing of an organic nature, I hope," I replied.

Our young friend bent down to sniff the grime. "They smell more like paint than anything else."

"Thank goodness."

"Still, it's a slap in the face to the script," said Wade.

"At this point, I don't care. We're not doing this for my ego. This is for Guy and his parents."

My angel tensed, like a man in need of a joint.

"Are you okay?"

"I'll be all right, Adam," he replied.

"Come on, Guy. You always want me to talk things over. What's on your mind?"

"There's so much going through my mind at the moment, where do I start?" His wings lowered. "Tonight, if all goes right, I'm meeting two people I always thought I'd never meet. Yet here I am in a bad cardigan about to gamble that meeting."

I wrapped my arms around him from behind.

"And I'm trying so hard not to think about meeting them and just to concentrate on going out there and doing the best performance I can." His eyes watered. "But yet again I'm only a bit player. Most of this play is between Mannix and Wade. Ziggy and I are just the dressing. The background props, if you like. It says a lot about my life in general."

Guy looked to the floor as the rest of us shared discreet glances.

Eventually Wade broke the silence. "And as you're one of my husband's best friends, I'm going to put on a performance that will get your parents out of here for good."

"Me too," said Mannix.

"And if not," the angel continued, "don't sweat it. It was never meant to be."

"INDULGE ME," SAID Preston.

This request was made as my actors were taking their places on set. A dining table that would have been refused by a secondhand charity store stood onstage. And the chairs were mismatched, with Wade seated slightly higher than everyone else. This must have stroked his ego.

The crowd sat waiting, most with arms folded. But at least there was light chatter. I knew we were going to win them over. I just knew it!

The Underworld leader waved me away from the makeshift stage toward an empty chair in the front row. I was slightly annoyed as I wanted to stay onstage and give a speech to welcome our audience myself. But he felt that was his role.

"My dear citizens, you're in for a treat tonight, I hope. In our conference room, we have the gift of theater. Some say it's the gift that keeps on giving, but we'll see if there's truth in that shortly."

Wade's eyes widened as he shared my glance, while Guy seemed nauseous, swaying on his seat.

"As you heard this afternoon at our lecture on insecurity, artists possess it in droves. And here is your homework, my friends; watch for those cracks."

I jumped up and spoke. "But it's those insecurities I'm sure you all know. Some hide behind outlandish fashion." I gestured at Preston. "Some hide behind authority. But we all have them in some way or another. And we'll keep having them until the end of time."

I sat. The pearl-wearing devil grunted before leaving us to do the play. I was relieved he wasn't staying.

"What do you mean you're leaving me?" Wade scowled as Angela.

"I'm bored," replied my angelic Cecil.

"Who is she?"

"There's no one else."

"What am I going to do for money?"

There was no laugh.

"Maybe you can marry Tony?" suggested Trevor's Mary. His monster wig made him look like a reject from *The Addams Family* casting.

"He's poor."

"But he's famous. It's only a matter of time before he makes some money out of it."

Again, no laugh. My heart sunk.

"What about Carter?" asked Mannix's Ronny. "He's loaded!"

"But look at his connections," Cecil sniped. "At least I'm leaving you instead of hiring a hit man to dispose of you."

Around the room were a few murmurs, but no mirth. The ragged-haired woman next to me yawned. The seed had been planted by Preston. Guy's parents were going nowhere.

"You realize, Mary, you'll have to stay naked until the reporters arrive," proclaimed Angela.

Cecil winked at Mary as she turned to Ronny in abject terror.

"Help!" Mary gasped like a damsel in distress.

Not a hoot nor a snicker. The audience was less enthusiastic than a room full of corpses. Even Trevor's campy hair couldn't save the day.

The scene ended, so Guy and Mannix made their way to the temporary greenroom that Preston had provided. It was a small tent to the side of the stage. I joined them as Wade and Trevor played the next scene.

"You'd swear we were putting on the *Amateur-ville Horror*," Mannix whispered.

"When the world says you're not good enough, get a second opinion," I replied.

"Adam, when Hell says you're not good enough, there is no second opinion."

Our angel quivered. I placed my arm around him.

"You're not saying much, Guy."

"What can I say? My parents will never make it out of here."

Mannix hugged our shell-shocked friend as his wings rose and fell. Onstage, Wade was trying a mannish voice for Angela, and his character talked about skipping past the sanitary pads in her local store, now that menopause had arrived. This was not in the script, but the script didn't work. Trevor sounded even campier as he ad-libbed about his wild sex drive. I peeked into the crowd. More of them had their arms folded.

Preston wandered down the aisle toward our tent with Josh ambling directly behind. They were drawing attention to themselves, but the Underworld figure didn't seem to care.

"Guy's not in the play for a while, is he?" he asked.

"No," I replied. "Why?"

"I think he needs to meet his parents."

He took the angel by the hand and promptly marched him away from us. As his boyfriend tried to follow, I grabbed his arm.

"Josh, clarify something for me."

"What, Adam?"

"You never wanted Guy to be in this play, did you? In fact, I don't think you ever wanted him to know about this deal with Preston."

"How did you know?"

"It's obvious," Mannix replied. "You kept his parents' whereabouts secret. You wanted Adam to get here so he could help without Guy ever knowing. But I blurted it out."

The demon nodded.

"But there's one thing I don't get," I said. "Why did you tell Guy about his parents in the first place? It's only caused him misery and a dope habit. Why didn't you wait until I got to the Afterlife and just include me in your plans?"

"I didn't have a plan because I let the cat out of the bag shortly after I met Guy again. You know the scenario. Romantic dinner. Too much wine. Loose lips." His bat wings shuddered. "So I promised myself not to let him know his parents were here while I negotiated their release." He turned to leave.

"One more thing," said Mannix. "Why haven't you had sex with him yet?"

"I have to go. I'm worried about Guy."

He rushed out.

Chapter Twenty-Six

"THIS CROWD HAS been lulled into boredom for so long, you'd swear they had lobotomies," said Trevor.

He and Mannix were with me in the tent as Wade was losing the audience in a scene where he was on the phone to Cecil. They discussed their long line of bedroom toys, which again was not in the script. I thought my husbands ad-libbing was hilarious. Sadly, only my cohorts agreed.

"I have an idea," I said. "Take your shirt off, Mannix."

"What?" he replied.

"Better still, take your clothes off."

"Adam, shouldn't we try to rescue the play's artistic integrity?"

"Wade's in a bad dress, and the audience needs stimuli."

It didn't take Mannix long to see my point, and I was glad to see his after so long. The basic charm that he exuded when I first met him posing nude for my art class was there in all its pleasing glory.

"Let's hope it's enough to win over the crowd," Trevor said. He took a second look. "It's enough to win me over!"

As Mannix walked back toward the performance space, Trevor and I tumbled out of the tent and strolled to the back of the audience to watch the play. When Wade saw our naked friend, his expression simulated a skydiver whose parachute didn't open.

I waved my arms behind the back row, trying to get my husband's attention. He noticed me as I walked around, swaying my hips while grabbing my imaginary boobs. Now he looked at me like the same skydiver about the hit the ground. I tried to whisper "Camp it up," but he shrugged. Soon Mannix was looking in my direction as well. Then the audience stared at me. Again I mouthed the words "Camp it up."

"Ramp it up where?" called Wade out loud.

Mannix froze. I briefly pictured a badly attired cross-dresser bonking a well-endowed young man. Bring back Herb Alpert and the Tijuana Brass as the porn soundtrack and we'd really have a show these punters would never forget.

"He means 'Camp it up,'" Trevor yelled.

"Oh," Wade replied.

My partner began to flounce.

"You are a very sexy young man," said Angela. The audience cheered as Wade brought on the spirit of Eartha Kitt without the credibility. "Don't let anyone tell you otherwise. I don't think my husband needs to know a thing."

"I think your husband is a very lucky man," replied the naked boy toy. He was trying not to laugh with the audience.

"Don't you want to find out how lucky he is?" Wade drooled.

He was pulling off high camp in a low seductive tone.

"Your actors are turning into Quentin Crisp to save the play," Trevor said.

"Some more than others," I replied, patting his wig.

"I'm not that experienced," Ronny confessed.

"I don't believe that for a minute," Angela replied.

Catcalls and whistles filled the room. Wade was the seductress gone wrong, and Mannix was the plaything trying to get his dignity back, and best of all, the seated zombies were lapping it up! There was no way Guy's parents wouldn't be allowed to leave this hellhole.

"Trev, I mean, Ziggy, stay here and do whatever you can to keep the laughter going. Go and compete for Ronny's affections if you have to."

"You want me naked as well?"

"If you need to, pull out all stops. Sophistication is not an option."

"Where are you going?"

"To find the others."

After reaching a few dead ends, I finally located yet another room as inspired as a wart. It was a dining area I'd never encountered during my solo stay, with the type of long tables and benches I'd expect in a medieval monks' monastery. There was a kitchen behind a rectangular hole in the wall where two uninspired inhabitants were cooking some sickly slop in huge pots. And it smelled bad. Imagine the odor of red cabbage boiled in vinegar and you get the idea. I prayed this wasn't our after-show catering.

But the real find were the cooks. They had wings, which, sadly, drooped like soggy tissue. The male was gray-haired, leather-faced, and had a meek stature. He wore a faraway expression, but I was sure he'd done this task a thousand times before. There was nothing left in his imagination to make it inspiring.

The older female angel was at his side. Her attitude was as lost as his. She stirred one of the pots with a wooden spoon and smiled at her male counterpart from time to time. Her long white hair lay against her wings like knotted cobweb. Her pale pink dress was frayed and slightly ripped. Like him, her best days had passed her by.

"Are you..." I stopped midsentence. Maybe there were a few fallen angels hanging around down here. I shouldn't have been making assumptions.

"Are we what?" the woman asked.

"Do you know Guy?"

Grins as proud as punch filled their faces. "You know our son," said the man, humbly.

"Well, of course. That's why I'm here. This is a big day for you."

"Why?" Guy's mum asked.

"It's your last day in the Underworld."

They looked at each other blankly.

"We're doing a play in the conference hall as payment for your release. Guy is taking you with him after we're done."

They chuckled helplessly to each other. "Is this a promise from Preston?" Guy's father asked.

"Yes. That's what he said. We do the play; Guy takes you home. Didn't he mention it?"

"You expect him to keep his word?"

"Well, he made a deal with your son's boyfriend."

"How sweet, Guy's got a boyfriend."

"Didn't he tell you?"

They stared at each other. "We haven't seen Guy since he was a baby," his mum confessed.

"But Preston said he was bringing Guy to meet you."

"Guy's here?"

"Yes, he's here!"

They turned down the hot plates and marched out of their nook. Both parents took me by the arm and strutted toward the next room.

"By the way, what are your names?" I asked.

"Eleanor and Alexander," the mum replied. "A rather pissed-off Eleanor and Alexander!"

"I'm Adam. A rather confused Adam."

In another room, the sound of honky-tonk piano was wafting through the air. The tune sounded like "Bill Bailey, Won't You Please Come Home," with a few errant notes. There were some people snoozing on the hard floor without anything to soften their slumber. Not even mattresses or yoga mats. At least the bad music would have bored them into a deep sleep.

"Preston, for the thousandth time, I'm not having sex with you!" yelled Guy's muffled voice from another room.

"You'll cave in. I'm like the man with the amyl bottle in the sauna. I'm the one in control."

We opened the door to find this was another entrance to Preston's bedroom.

"What are you doing to our son?" Eleanor roared.

Preston was wearing a studded leather harness and black leather pants. His pearls and top hat were still locked in place. Fortunately, Guy hadn't lost his jeans, but his bad cardigan had lost some buttons. He huddled close to one of the blood-red pillows. I briefly imagined Preston's entire harem getting up to all sorts of mischief in this huge bed, and still having enough room to sleep comfortably. I thought of those poor devils outside asleep on the floor, while comfort was nearby.

My angel noticed his parents and briefly looked as happy as a child discovering their Christmas presents under the tree. Someone grunted behind me. It was Josh tied and gagged to a chair.

"Adam, go back to your play," the Underworld leader said. "Let the adults have fun." He glared at us like the Captain reprimanding the Von Trapp kids.

"Preston, darling," mother angel responded, "are you threatening innocent bystanders again?"

"Eleanor, I gave intimidation up for Lent."

"If you lay one hand on my son, I'll nail you to a cross!"

I began to untie Josh, but our villain marched toward us. Eleanor helped me as Alexander spread his wings in anger.

"You don't have the authority to free us," Guy's father stated.

"He doesn't?" queried our ungagged demon buddy.

"What do you mean he doesn't?" I asked. "Why are we doing the play then?"

"It doesn't matter what he promised," the dad continued. "If that devil so much as lays a kiss on our son's lips, Guy will be trapped in the Underworld!"

As Preston pushed Alexander aside and reached for Eleanor, Joshua stood free. But it was Guy who grabbed the leader by his pearls and swung him so they stood face-to-face. The angel's wings expanded to full glory, before he used their feathered tips to poke at Preston's chest. Then he stepped toward him while at the same time pushing him into a corner of the bedroom.

Josh was about to help, but I gestured him back. He saw my point. Even the parents let Guy find an inner strength that had gone astray.

"So Mr. High and Mighty," he roared, "you were going to keep me here as one of your minions! What did you think I'd do? Worship you like a god? Fall from grace just for your entertainment?" Now his wings latched themselves under the leather straps of Preston's fetish wear and lifted him to the ceiling. "No one treats me or my friends as personal playthings. If you need reassurance about your status, then go back to your mindless harem!"

Preston cowered like a sitting duck about to be shot by a crazed hunter.

"Guy, maybe you should let him down," his father said.

The good son looked at Alexander with a wicked grin, before flinging the scumbag onto the bed. He bounced gracelessly on the velvet bedspread before thumping his skull on the headboard.

"I get the message," Preston uttered. "I'm bowing out of this situation with dignity." He clutched his chest. "I still have my pearls."

"Let's leave this loser alone," I said.

I went to grab Guy's hand, but his parents beat me to it. The three walked out of the bedroom arm in arm as Josh and I followed. We tiptoed past the sleeping souls back toward the conference area.

"That was a close call, my son," said Alexander.

"If you went a step further, you would've been here with us," Eleanor added.

"So let me get this straight," I said. "Preston's seed mixed with an angel damns that angel to the Underworld. Am I right?"

"Even a demon's seed does the same thing," she replied.

"And how come Guy didn't know this?"

"It's not something many angels know. After all, angels don't often have sex with Underworld beings."

Their son turned to Josh as a lightbulb lit up above my head. I now knew why they hadn't made love.

Guy pulled at the buttonholes of his cardigan, keeping it wrapped around his body. "Then that means..." he began.

Alexander and Eleanor stopped to exchange coy glances. We all halted.

"Was it worth it?" I asked.

"*It* was," replied Eleanor gleefully.

"What followed wasn't," her loving partner replied. "Our three-way led to being prisoners."

"And the offspring are damned to make the same mistakes as their parents," Guy remarked.

"Does that mean...?" My voice trailed off.

"No," replied Eleanor. "Guy is not the result of our ménage à trois. He was still a baby when our experimental stage blossomed. But our demon lover suggested that the three of us raise him down here, in the Underworld. We could never let that happen, so we left him with our friend, Aunt Jemima."

"Once we were free to go," Alexander continued, "we went in search of Aunt Jemima. But she was no longer part of the Afterlife. We asked around, but no one seemed to know where Guy was. Eventually, we came back here."

"Hold on," said Guy. "You can leave. But weren't you damned to stay here?"

"For a while. But after that time, we were free to go."

"Hold on!" My mind was working overtime. "This doesn't make sense. If you were damned to stay, how could you drop Guy off with Aunty Jemima? Who told you about the demon/angel seed mixing rule?"

"Preston did."

"He told me the same thing," Joshua professed.

"I see what you're getting at, Adam," said Guy. "It sounds like a bad lie.

Like the lie of making a deal to rescue my parents by putting on a play."

"I want to go back and deck him!"

"Calm down, Josh," I said. "Poor Mannix, Ziggy, and Wade have been pulling out all stops to entertain that unspirited lot."

"Which is why we returned to the Underworld," said Eleanor. "This is a place of lost souls. One by one, we help them get out of here."

"Angels to the core. And Guy continues that cause with those upstairs."

Alexander pointed upward. "You're still...?"

"Where else would he be?"

"Adam told us you had a boyfriend," said Eleanor.

"I have," Guy replied hesitantly.

"What's he like?"

"Tall. Charismatic. But most of all, he's there for me."

"And he's a handsome devil," she said. "Even with his fine demon wings."

"You knew?" Guy and Joshua asked in unison.

"I worked it out when you gave him that subtle look of love. A mother knows. I can't say I approve."

"Yes, son." The father was weighing in. "Don't repeat the sins of your parents. And besides, only Preston enjoys the vices on offer. You'd be bored."

"But like we discussed before, what if mixing seed with a demon is just a myth?" I said.

The others continued to walk as I followed.

"No, seriously. Think this through."

But they were preoccupied.

"We love you, Guy," his mother said. "We know you won't do anything stupid."

"And we're very proud of you, Guy," his father added.

"I don't want to leave you," their son replied.

"You can visit us. After all, you have a demon boyfriend. He can guide you here and take you back home."

We got to the door of the conference room. I wanted to be angry as I tried to work out how much of this was a sham. But seeing my friend's family reunited took any doubt that just being here, whatever the reason, was worth it.

"Adam, we can't leave now," Guy pleaded.

"Stay here and talk," I replied. "When you're all ready, come and watch the end of the play before we say our good-byes."

I blew them all a quick kiss and went inside.

The audience were still having a ball. I stood next to Trevor at the back, watching with glee. Mannix played Ronny both coyly and shamelessly. At times butter wouldn't melt in his mouth. At other moments, it would sizzle. Wade purred like Catwoman trying to get into Batman's utility belt.

"Three aces or a royal flush?" the onstage hussy asked.

"What do you mean by the poker reference?" our naked buddy replied.

"You seem to hold your cards close to your chest."

"How so?"

"You hint at a chance to get neighborly." She started chasing him around the stage area. "Then you retract the offer when I'm willing to cash in my gift voucher."

Mannix ran down the aisle; all components flopping aimlessly. The crowd clapped.

"We're good neighbors," he replied. "We have an excellent relationship."

"But you know and I know, we both want more."

Wade had lust in his eyes.

The fun went on for another fifteen minutes or so. As the applause began, I noticed Guy, Joshua, Alexander, and Eleanor at the opposite corner of the conference room.

"The parents we heard so much about," said Mannix. He strolled toward the angel family, forgetting he was naked.

"The one and only," replied Guy. "Alexander and Eleanor, this is Mannix."

"A fine young man," said Eleanor as she shook his hand.

Reality hit him as he looked down to see his crown jewels. But the crowd were exiting between him and the tent where his clothes were. He shrugged and shook Alexander's hand.

"It's my pleasure," the young man said. "Guy's wanted to meet you both for as long as I've known him."

Wade and Trevor, or Ziggy as he was pretending to be, introduced themselves as well. As for me, well, I wanted to get out of there and never see the place again.

"Do you want to join us for a drink, Alexander? Eleanor?" I asked. "I think all of us need one. Especially your son."

"Now, Adam, we're bound by duty," replied the maternal angel. The family group hugged.

"Maybe I should stay," murmured my guardian in the middle of his cuddle.

"Guy, you have important work to do," his mother replied. "You need to go without us."

"No, I'm staying here."

"Guy, is that wise?" Mannix asked.

"Yes, Guy. Think of all those badly synthesized hits from yesteryear you'll have to listen to," I said. "And the insipid color schemes in most of the rooms are enough to make you wish you were color blind."

"Adam's right," Eleanor added. "And wait till you taste the food."

"It can't be that bad," said Guy.

"Imagine meat so rancid that even the cockroaches keep away from the kitchen."

"And broth so bland you wish you were eating dog food just for the aftertaste," added Alexander.

"We know. We're the cooks."

"They're right," I said. "I've stayed here. Let your parents save these souls from eternal monotony. You save the souls in the Afterlife."

I couldn't read my angel's expression.

"You need to go, son," his mother said. "Otherwise you'll *all* end up staying here."

"Now go with peace of mind," was his dad's blessing.

Joshua and I took him by the hand, but he broke free to give his parents one last hug.

Eleanor clutched her son so tight I'd swear he was about to choke. Alexander looked on silently. Tears welled in all members of the family. But they didn't weep. Only several drops wet their faces. *Perhaps Guy is crying out for air?*

His dad now held him while his mother stood with eyes closed. *Is she replaying their last touch in her mind?* The men remained cheek to cheek for some time, savoring their lost years.

Mannix took this opportunity to grab his clothes. Then we bid Guy's parents farewell and headed for the next room. As we opened the door, Eleanor and Alexander blew their son a kiss. Guy smiled like a boy discovering Santa.

Chapter Twenty-Seven

"A TOAST TO Eleanor and Alexander!"

With a champagne glass held high, Guy spoke louder than he had to, gaining the attention of several other patrons at the Carousel. But his pride was infectious.

"We'll *all* drink to that," I replied.

"Now that they know where you are, I'll bet anything they'll leave the Underworld and make up for lost years," said Wade.

"That crossed my mind too," Mannix said. Guy seemed to ponder.

The bar was crowded that night. A ramshackle cast gossiped noisily in their distinct groups. A small faction dressed in multifaith religious wear also raised their glasses with us. The bearded man in a nun's outfit yelled something unintelligible before gulping down his beer, while a plump woman in a Buddhist monk's robe sang unrelated lines from *The Sound of Music*.

They brought kids with them who ran around the room, discovering the assorted toys on the other tables. Curiosity made me look down to ours. It was a tin rocket in blue and silver. I spun it. It whizzed off its axis and finally stopped, pointing at Wade. He didn't notice.

"Can we go back and visit Preston's harem?" said Trevor. "I want to reserve the one with the crooked nose."

"I noticed him too," Wade replied. "But he needs to be put on lay-by for a few years."

"He's the right age for me," said Mannix.

"You're taken," I reminded him.

"What's good for the goose..."

"Oh brother." I cringed. "All we need now is to all laugh uncontrollably and we've got the ending to a bad movie."

Bongos began to play. The beatnik was here again, and I pointed him out to Joshua who was in his angel disguise. Fortunately, the hippy wasn't reciting this time. He was joined by two pals who swayed drowsily with each beat.

"Hello, beautiful." We turned toward the voice. It was David with a single red rose in his hand. Mannix's grin was so large you could have played piano on his teeth. They kissed like lovers who lived on different continents and hadn't seen each other in years.

"Romance is in the air," I said.

Wade nodded gently.

"Where's Guy's parents?" David asked.

"I'll fill you in later," Mannix replied. "Let me get you a drink."

Our friend strolled past the beatnik and his followers before stopping. He stepped backward to take a closer look. He then promptly turned and headed back to us.

"Why didn't you get David a drink?" I asked.

"It's Mary."

"Where?" He pointed to the tubbier of the two robe-wearing hippies.

Tie up your shoelaces.
Leave nothing to chance.
For if you leave spaces,
There'll be no way to advance.

Just when we thought it was safe, bongo man struck.

"What's he on about now?" Josh asked.

"What's he on is the real question," I replied.

Leave no friend behind.
Leave no lover behind.
But finish your drinks before you leave.

For some reason, it was Mary who recited that last verse.

"She's not bad," said Guy.

"Leave no lover behind," Wade repeated. "I guess there's wisdom in her words."

David kissed Mannix, then gave my husband a knowing look.

"Do it now," he said to my Wade.

"Do what now?" I asked.

My partner kissed my forehead, then told me to step outside with him. We walked to the exit, but I kept an eye on Trevor's body language, looking for clues.

It was a cloudless night. Wade's chocolate eyes displayed a warmth that had been missing for ages. He reached for my hands. I held *his* willingly.

"Adam, when did you first know I really loved you?"

"When you threw out your old love letters. That was commitment. That was when I knew there was no one else but me."

"Do you want to know when I first realized I loved you?"

I smiled.

"That first kiss over dinner. I was held in suspended animation, eager for the next taste of your lips."

"Wade, when did you become so poetic?"

"Maybe that crazed beatnik inside is casting a spell on me. Or maybe all that ad-libbing in the play has freed my creative juices. But one thing I know for sure, Adam, tonight I was proud of you."

"Proud of me?" I was feeling teary but held back the waterworks.

"What you did for Guy was impressive."

"Wade, we all did it for Guy. Even if it was a waste of time."

"No, Adam. The roles were reversed. You became *his* guardian angel."

"So I was a saint tonight. I wasn't a saint before I died."

"My husband, we've shared too much history for me to let you go. I forgive you."

"And I'm so sorry for what happened, Wade."

"You've apologized already, Adam."

"But I don't feel like I can say it enough."

He eased me toward him. We kissed. No murmurs from passersby made it to my ears. No footsteps traced a path down the street. This world had politely frozen time, just for us. The taste of my man bewitched me with a long-absent charm I forgot I was addicted to. In a daze, I moved away.

"This is a dumb question to ask, Wade, especially as everything is perfect, but I need to know. When did you decide to forgive me? Was it during the play?"

"A little before. Trevor gave me some perspective."

My jaw dropped. "You know about him. You know he's not Ziggy!"

"Yes. I've known for some time."

"When did you suspect?"

"When he was over for dinner. I worked it out early in the night. That's why I seemed confused."

"You seemed a bit lost, but I wouldn't say you were confused."

"Okay, but you obviously noticed."

"Are you kidding? I was guilt central!"

"I guess we both suffered that night, Adam." He kissed me on the forehead. "But Mannix said some things that evening that made me think about our marriage. I saw us through someone else's eyes."

"In a way, he has insider knowledge."

"He was spot-on when he spoke about the way we work together. We're a team, Adam, we're a team." He tilted his head. "Plus, I got tired of feeling angry."

I wiped a tear from my cheek. "Hold on a second. If you worked out who Ziggy was early that night, why were you so chummy with him when we were in the Underworld?"

"Hey, he does drag well. And he's fun. I can't dislike the guy. He's so damn likable."

"Wow, my saving grace is a likeable slut."

"Oh yes. He confessed a lot." He shook his head while grinning wholeheartedly. "You had some quirky Fifth Dimension meetings. I should have joined you."

"Don't say that, Wade. I have you back." I kissed him briefly. "Let's just make this adventure about you and me from now on."

"I'll toast to that. But I want to apologize as well."

"About what?"

"About not believing in your guardian angel."

"We've already had this conversation at the Valley of Lost Loves."

"Adam, I'm feeling a need to repeat myself. Let me."

"No need. I wouldn't have believed that story either if I were in your shoes. I'd probably think I was going mad too."

He smirked.

"I forgive you for thinking I was losing the plot."

"That's why you looked for people as mad as you."

"Wade, from now on, only you are as mad as me."

Another lingering kiss. His tongue danced with mine, knowing every step. My heart was his again, protected by his love.

"I don't want to go back inside," I whispered.

"We can't just leave, Adam."

We looked through the doorway. My angel had a reserved dignity I hadn't seen for ages, like a king who knew his loyal subjects would lay down their lives at any time, just for him.

"You're right, Wade. It is Guy's night, after all. But I want tonight to be special for us as well. I know! I'll cook pasta when we get home. I want a romantic dinner before we go to bed."

"But it'll be late, Adam. And you always overcook pasta. The water bubbles out of the pot because you get bored keeping an eye on it."

"I'm not that bad. What about you? Remember the time you made pasta for our friends and you underestimated just how much dried linguine expands? You used every bowl we had to serve dinner. Plus we had leftovers all week."

We giggled like teenagers. He held me closer. His scent refreshed me like a warm shower. His next kiss reminded me to never let go.

"We should go back in, Wade."

"I'm in no rush."

But I pecked him on the cheek before we took our first step toward the door. We halted when we noticed Guy was coming to join us.

"This is your night," I said.

"But it should be yours, Adam," he replied.

I looked at Wade. "It is. It definitely is." We briefly kissed again. "Guy, what are you talking about? You met your parents. This is *your* night."

"Should I join the others?" Wade asked. "This sounds like a private conversation."

"Stay," the angel replied. "I need to show you something."

With one raised wing, we were somewhere I didn't want to be. In front of us was Trevor and me in his lounge room, talking, yet our voices were muted.

"I don't want to be here," my husband asserted.

"Wade and I have made up," I said to Guy. "This is not helping our reconciliation."

"Hold on," the angel said. "You know what I'm about to show you, Wade?"

"Yes, I do. It's the night Adam and Trevor were murdered."

"You know he's not Ziggy?"

Wade nodded.

"Wow. So we kept the charade up for nothing." Guy snapped his fingers and instantly the scene before us paused. "I know this seems cruel, but hear me out. Adam, you were right. I wasn't keeping an eye on you during your final few weeks. I was peeping, but not watching."

"That's why I arrived on the conveyor belts," I said. "So out of guilt you kept an eye on Wade, and when it was his turn, you organized our private meeting."

"Conveyor belts?" my husband asked.

"I'll explain later."

"Because I didn't see you die, Adam, I decided I should sort out the facts," the angel continued. "If I'm any sort of guardian at all, I have to be clear."

"You're still talking riddles."

"The scene you're about to watch is different than you think. Even Trevor hasn't seen it, or hasn't fully remembered it. As far as he knows, he was your lover, Adam."

"He was at some stage, like the rest of the group."

Guy was shaking his head. "You see, I watched you arrive at the meetings. I watched you leave with whoever you were assigned to that night. But I didn't watch you beyond that. I couldn't. I knew you were doing it to connect with me, and I knew what it was doing to Wade."

"For a guardian angel, your timing is way off. Wade and I were making up and you come out of the pub and—"

Guy snapped his fingers.

"Adam, if you don't have sex with the others, you won't find the Fifth Dimension." Trevor was stern in his tone, like a boss about to fire an employee.

"Everyone's been gossiping," I murmured, sounding defeated. "I guess I couldn't get away with it forever. But at least I was naked for the meditation."

"But you've got to have sex! Our bodies need to have that intense connection. Together we become one entity as we turn each other on. Bear ourselves to our group." He shook his head. "You know this, Adam. Why am I repeating myself? You should have done this every time you went home with someone."

"Hey, I stripped. We were naked, chanting. That ought to be enough."

"You're getting a reputation, Adam."

"I know. For not sleeping around."

"You can both close your mouths," the angel said.

"Guy, I've been through hell while I've been here thinking that..." I couldn't finish my sentence.

"I think it's, it's..." Wade laughed as he paused. "It's adorable."

"Adorable?"

"Yeah, Adam. Adorable. We were distant, but you still didn't seek affection. Now I'm the guilty one for thinking..." He laughed again.

"I, um, I, um, don't know what to say." I took the longest breath before I started to giggle. "I'm speechless. Angry, but speechless." But I was talking through my chuckles. Yes, I was mad at Guy, but a weight had lifted, more than it had while Wade and I were making up.

"Oh dear," said Wade. His laughter stopped. "This is when it happened."

"Strip!"

This was not Trevor's voice. In the ghostly echo from the past, my Fifth Dimension mentor was visually shaken. I seemed confused until gradually my eyes also widened in terror.

"Guy, stop the scene," I pleaded. "I'm remembering what happened. I don't need to see it."

"Hush, Adam dear," he replied. "This part is for Wade. It's what he needs to know."

"How did you get in?" Trevor asked. "I didn't hear—"

"I've been lying under your bed since five p.m." A man in his thirties stood trembling. His face as crazed as a prisoner that no one visited. Knotted hair, a crumpled shirt, and rubber boots were secondary to the large carving knife in his hand.

"Who are you?" the vision of me whimpered.

"Adam," Trevor began, "meet my ex."

Guy raised his wing and instantly we were back outside the Carousel.

The others were enjoying themselves inside. I fell into Wade's arms, not really knowing how I felt.

"Thank you," my husband said. "Thank you for showing me the truth. I was stupid to think my Adam would ever—"

"Wade, it's okay," I replied. "It just shows how much I mean to you."

We stayed in our embrace for what felt like an eternity. My love and I saying so much in our silence. I was home. There were no skeletons in my closet, and I had Guy to thank for letting us both know. I finally understood why he used that moment to reveal what he had only just worked out for himself. I couldn't be mad at him. He was my guardian.

And like a good angel, he quietly slipped away, giving Wade and I more time to just be. The love of my lives would always be there, no matter what would follow.

Eventually, we joined the others, walking hand in hand as we entered the pub.

The secret is in our passing.
That's where the mystery unfolds.
Behind the veil, between the lesson and the eternal.

"But he's got a point," said Trevor.

"Who's got a point?" Wade asked.

Trevor pointed to the beatnik.

"Bongo-man's got a point?

"Hear me out. The beatnik said 'the secret is in our passing.' He's been saying that over and over again in different verses." Trevor paused as Guy, Mannix, and David rested their champagne glasses on the table. "Let's look at how we all passed. Adam, you and I were murdered by my crazed ex. I've got other mates here who've also died in bizarre ways. One had a bungee-jumping accident. Another got depressed and topped himself. And another died in a car crash."

"Trevor's onto something I've never considered," I said. "Mannix, you *also* died in a car crash."

"And I died of a heart attack," Wade added.

"Or a broken heart," I replied.

He kissed me tenderly.

"And I died of peanuts in my cupcake," said David.

"Peanuts?" I queried. "Wasn't it a poison cupcake from a double-agent drag queen?"

He smirked. "Not quite. More of the memory has been flooding back."

"He was playing a virtual reality game," Mannix clarified.

"And during the chase from the firing plane, my friend offered me a chocolate and peanut cupcake."

"And he's allergic to peanuts."

"So I choked with my computer headwear on."

"See!" Trevor shrieked. "Everyone here died before their time. So where are those people who simply died of old age? Guy, only you would know."

The mystery unfolds as truths get told.

The bongo player ended his recital with a drum roll. Mary clapped. He stood and bowed before tapping his instrument lightly. At this point, the annoying Christian spotted us and leapt up. She ran toward me with the speed of a bowling ball. Her arms opened wide and clutched me like an octopus about to feed.

"I'm sorry, Adam."

I reluctantly patted her head. "You're sorry for what?"

She stepped away. "For being such a damn fool to you and your friends."

"Hey, you looked after my culinary habits in the Underworld. You weren't that much of a fool."

"No, I was. I lived as a fool. I was one of the masses who never questioned, when the person I needed to question ended the life of my precious boy. So I died a fool."

"Whoa. You've been doing some serious self-reflection."

"Then I literally had to go to Hell to sort myself out." She looked to the others. "So I'm sorry to all of you for judging. It's the shortcomings of a gal who never expanded her horizons."

"Only the ignorant invent their enemies," said Guy.

She looked to the bongo player. "I vow never to be ignorant again."

"I never thought I'd say this to you, Mary." I placed my hand on her shoulder. "I'm proud of you." I moved my hand away, then high-fived her.

The beatnik played passionately again as the multifaith patrons danced around him. Mary blew me a kiss as she joined the tribal mob.

Behind the veil, between the lesson and the eternal,

is where the mystery unfolds and the truth is told.

Children ran around the revelers with toy planes, flying them to imaginary locations. I picked up the tin rocket again. I could have sworn it vibrated, about to take off while still in my hand and take me to uncharted territory.

"Guy, what's bongo-man trying to say with his mumbo jumbo about the truth and the eternal?" Trevor asked.

The angel shrugged.

"Okay, to put it bluntly, what is the meaning of life?"

"Yeah, Guy," said Wade. "Who wins in the game of life? Is it lovers like us, or free spirits like Trevor?"

"Oh dear," said Joshua. "It's philosophy o'clock."

"It's the one with the most mourners at their funeral," Mannix replied.

"How do you know?" I asked.

"Adam, I've been welcoming lost souls with Guy. I'm in on his secrets. Well, some of them, anyway. I never made the connection that everyone here has died prematurely."

"And what other secrets are here?" I asked. "Guy, for an angel who's always guided me through life, you're terribly quiet now."

A dance beat boomed through my senses. I tapped my foot. Wade also moved to the thumping tune.

"What's that music?" my husband asked.

Even Trevor and Mannix jigged a little.

"And why are we the only ones who can hear it?" I queried.

Bongo-man was still playing while his new followers continued swaying. And a woman with amazing heels got up and danced to his beat, oblivious to the techno.

As usual, the barmaid brought drinks to the patrons, and a middle-aged gent argued that he didn't have enough to drown his sorrows. She returned with a pitcher.

One of the kids ran up to me so I gave her my rocket. This lucky red-haired girl charged back and ran circles around the beatnik with her toy held high.

A baby was held in deep slumber. A woman tried putting makeup on her friend. A couple gazed into each other's eyes as if Cupid had just struck.

But there was no sign of other people hearing the music.

Guy lifted his glass. "I'm toasting your lives. Raise your drinks with me."

We did.

"Some people have just disappeared," Trevor shrieked. "And Joshua is in his demon form."

"I'm testing something," Joshua responded.

"That doesn't explain why people have disappeared."

"They're muses," I replied. Guy's eyebrows lifted. "They're not like us. They're not lost souls. They're the supporting cast, or the fictional characters, who guide the rest of us back to where we should be."

"Adam, what's going on?" Wade asked.

"It's something I learned from Guy long ago," I replied.

David and my husband stared at me like I had all the answers.

"But that's the only secret I know. As for everything else going on, I'm in the dark." I slapped my forehead. "Guy, come on, there's no time for riddles anymore. Why is no one freaking out at Josh in his demon form? And what's that music?"

"Hey, the bongo player just disappeared as well," Trevor cried.

"Wow. He was our cosmic messenger, I think. Guy, what's going on?"

My guardian angel wrapped his wings around us all. A fanfare blew out of the dance beat, which soon morphed into the tune of the M People hit "One Night in Heaven." Then my angel lifted his wings.

"Welcome to the end of the game," he announced. "You don't have to pass Go and collect your properties. There's no more of life's snakes or ladders ahead of you. For your mortal lives are now complete. Eternity awaits!"

The pub and its patrons had disappeared, while a thick white fog came to encircle us.

"Guy, you never told me about any of this," Mannix complained.

"Yeah," said David. "How could you keep secrets like this from the man who helped you welcome the dead?"

"Because I had to make sure his soul was pure. I've had other people help me who ended up creating drama out of their own issues."

"Hey, there's no ground!" Trevor squealed.

"We're floating on air," I cried.

"I get it!" Wade shouted. "I get it!"

"What do you get?" I asked.

He pointed toward the music. "Over there is the promised land."

"No!" I was scratching my head. "Really? Then what was—?"

"Limbo," Guy replied.

"Limbo?" Mannix queried. "Yeah, I get in now. Limbo."

"Limbo," I said, feeling dizzy. Wade held me. "Oh dear, he's right. We all died too soon, so some of those people had muses to help them finish the lives they didn't." I scratched my head again. "Oh my, I hope Mary wasn't my muse."

"No, she wasn't," Guy replied. "But you helped her move a step closer to where she really wants to be." His wings fluttered thrice. "Perhaps you can take over my job?"

"No thanks. I tried welcoming new arrivals. It wasn't one of my best days."

"Everyone has experiences that leave a fingerprint or a bruise, Adam," my angel continued. "The trick is not to let them become scars."

David grabbed Trevor, who looked like he was about to faint. Mannix watched in deep thought, sharing his attention between his boyfriend and Guy.

"Welcome to the end of your factory reset," Joshua declared.

"That's why you ran away to the Underworld, Adam," my husband claimed.

"The Underworld?" I queried. "What has that got to do with anything?"

"Because the people in the Underworld have given up. They don't move forward. That's why Alexander and Eleanor stay there to help stagnant souls get back here so they can start moving onto that place there." He pointed ahead.

"Angels. Of course! Guy, you're the only angel here, except for your parents. The rest are probably where that music is coming from. Yet you fearlessly stay here to help us poor souls get to that music. Just like your parents, you stay here to help us!"

He took me from Wade's loving arms and held me tight.

"I'm sorry I wasn't more open with you about the true nature of this place, Adam. I wanted to be many times, but that would have stunted your growth. And it would have stunted your destiny with your soul mate."

"I need to go home to pack before we head to the music."

"No, Adam," my guardian replied. "No baggage allowed in the Promised Land."

Red and gold laser lights shot into the fog from the distance. Fierce female vocals soared above the sound of a reveling crowd. We were truly about to enter our version of Heaven.

I gazed romantically at Wade while still in my guardian's embrace.

"We've shared our lives," I recited, "and this time we sailed."

Sparks flew from Joshua's direction. Guy let go of me as we watched his boyfriend become shrouded by an intense glow. Soon he took on his angel disguise.

"Good to see you've changed your mind on your appearance," I said. "That's the best look for where we're obviously heading."

"This is not a disguise anymore," the demon replied.

"What do you mean?"

"Preston kept one of his promises."

I boogied a crazy dance of happiness on the spot.

"You really do want to live your life onstage, don't you?" said Joshua.

"Very funny." I grabbed him by the ears and pulled him to my lips, kissing him fleetingly. "What you and Preston have just done for Guy, well, it's, it's, it's more unselfish than us trying to free his parents with a play."

"Maybe I should change my name," said Mannix.

"Whatever for?" David asked.

"Mannix doesn't have a Heavenly ring to it."

We all groaned.

Guy snapped his fingers and champagne glasses appeared in our hands once more.

"A toast to your lives!" he declared. "To Trevor and his search for enlightenment. To Mannix and his successful search to unlock the nature of love. To David and his newfound wisdom not to take a new romance for granted. To Adam and Wade and their exploration of each other as soul mates. And last but not least, to Joshua, who has given me the greatest gifts. His love. His soul. And my parents."

"And to Guy," I added. "Like a true friend, he shows you your inner disco lights."

"Is that meant to be deep?" Josh asked.

"It's what comes to mind as I look into the distance."

"I think we got the best part of this deal," said David to Mannix.

"What do you mean?"

"I've only been here for a nanosecond compared to you and the others, yet here we are facing paradise."

We downed our champagne before our glasses magically refilled themselves. The thumping beat became louder as Guy took a step toward the tune. The mist was clearing. A quirky castle, which looked to be made of foamy white bubbles, opened its golden metal gates. Cheers roared above the pulsating rhythms, and if my eyes weren't playing tricks on me, I swore I saw glow sticks waved by hundreds through the haze.

Wade held my hand. Soon Guy held the other. His new angelic boyfriend walked beside him. Trevor grabbed Wade's spare hand as Mannix and David followed.

Ahead of us was the end of this tale. The after-party to our lives, if you like. And as welcoming as it looked, it was yet another chapter to face. More growth to endure. We'd celebrate tonight, and at some stage, we'd meet our maker. *Which god from my interfaith beliefs will greet us? Or will some unimaginable deity cast accusing glances at my misadventures?* No, of course not. I was worried about nothing.

But still, I halted. The others regarded me like a puzzle they had to solve. Wade and Guy let go of my hands. I grinned sheepishly. I'd become used to Limbo as my home, and now there was a new twist in the plot. Something else to get my head around.

"What's the matter, Adam," my husband asked.

Butterflies darted to the corners of my stomach. "I'm trying to deal with the fact that the Afterlife wasn't exactly the Afterlife, and as I look ahead, my curiosity is waning."

"I knew you'd do this. You're just scared."

"Well, curiosity killed the cat."

"But satisfaction brought it back," Guy added.

I looked at David and Mannix, holding hands like school kids about to skip along to class. Josh crossed his arms and eyed me up and down. But he had a right to judge as here he was, about to tread a new path as a new entity—a white-winged angel.

And once more, I gazed at my man, and I couldn't help think about the many times we'd fallen in love as completely different people, while guided by our supporting cast. Perhaps that's why the concept of reincarnation appeals to us with a thespian bent? We push ourselves onstage and find new things to say and new people to say them through. Our voice is guided by the souls who've lost in love, won a heart, or moved mountains.

And we learn to do this in life as well, so when we walk in someone else's shoes we take another step forward in unraveling the mystery of being human. Then we share this wisdom with others, and with our audience.

The music kept thumping as the roaring masses sang along, shouting each line of their Heavenly song. As I glanced at the castle, something rolled toward us in the distance like an anteater's tongue. It finally stopped at my feet.

"If that's not a sign, Adam, I don't know what is," my husband said.

A red carpet had made its way from the castle to us. I crouched and felt its lush surface, running my hands through the woolen strands. Then I rose and stepped forward, once again taking Wade and Guy by the hand.

"But where's the paparazzi?" Trevor asked.

"I was waiting for you to say that," my husband claimed.

"And I knew that's how you'd reply, my beautiful man," I said. We kissed.

Trevor soon walked without a playful stride. Josh lowered his angel wings and lost his devilish grin.

Mannix and David charged ahead, reminding me of our lost youth. I knew that like us, the jigsaw pieces of their personalities might not always connect, but in time, the edges would smooth to fit.

I tightened my grip on my husband and my angel. These were the two most precious people sharing my journey. I had been in their thoughts when I believed I'd been forgotten. And I yearned for them, not understanding that they hadn't given up on me. And through their eternal love, I understood the greatest mystery of all. Me.

After all, your costars hold a mirror to your soul.

About the Author

Kevin lives with his long-term partner, Warren, in their humble apartment (affectionately named Sabrina), in Australia's own 'Emerald City,' Sydney.

From an early age, Kevin had a passion for writing, jotting down stories and plays until it came time to confront puberty. After dealing with pimple creams and facial hair, Kevin didn't pick up a pen again until he was in his thirties. His handwritten manuscript was being committed to paper when his work commitments changed, giving him no time to write. Concerned, his partner, Warren, secretly passed the notebook to a friend who in turn came back and demanded Kevin finish his story. It wasn't long before Kevin's active imagination was let loose again.

His first novel spawned a secondary character named Guy, an insecure gay angel, but many readers argue that he is the star of the Actors and Angels book series. Guy's popularity surprised the author.

So with his fictional guardian angel guiding him, Kevin hopes to bring more whimsical tales of love, life and friendship to his readers.

Website: www.kevinklehr.com
Facebook: www.facebook.com/DramaQueensWithLoveScenes/
Twitter: @kevinklehr
Goodreads: www.goodreads.com/author/show/4298144.Kevin_Klehr
Vimeo: vimeo.com/companionmedia/
YouTube: www.youtube.com/channel/UCcJrnpZjgSjbpCiBp-pA3Jw/

Also by Kevin Klehr

Actors and Angels Series
Drama Queens with Love Scenes
Drama Queens and Adult Themes

From Top to Bottom

Nate and Cameron Series
Nate and the New Yorker
Nate's Last Tango

Recently Released from Kevin Klehr

Nate and the New Yorker

Nate and Cameron, Book 1

Chapter One

"I THINK PRAGUE is for lovers," said Ben. He'd just complained about how milky the coffee was in the Czech Republic, and now this. "Yeah. Prague is the place you take your one true love."

"Then what's Paris?" I asked.

"That's easy," replied Lucy. "Paris is where you have a steamy affair."

"Then I guess Amsterdam is for singles to get up to mischief," I added.

My friends stared into space as if they were pondering the meaning of life, while their goulash was getting cold. I looked at my food. The enticing mix of hearty cuisine slopped on my plate had me slobbering like a mutt. My knife cracked the surface of my deep-fried potato rösti, and as my fork made its way to my lips, it had to stop so I could take in the odor of this salty indulgence.

"Really, Nathan!" Lucy glared at me as if she was watching some kinky sex act even she'd disapprove of. "Just eat the bloody thing. I swear sex and food stimulate the same part of your brain."

I crunched hard, making sure my grin reached both ears. She rolled her eyes and shoved a huge chunk of carrot and beef in her mouth before smirking. Strange violin music came from above. As I glanced up at the tinny speaker, the middle-aged waitress who looked as if she should cut down on sampling the food sidled up to me.

"You like?"

She pointed to the speaker. I wanted to say it sounded like someone was murdering that musical instrument, but I decided to keep my mouth shut.

"My son. He practice music. Good, eh?" The three of us nodded. "I make louder." She marched away proudly.

"Eat quickly," said Ben. "That music sounds like someone is strangling a cat."

"I never pictured a woman her age wearing lilac," stated Lucy.

"Well, we are away from the tourist spots," I said. "You have to expect local charm when we eat in this district."

"And the food is better," said Ben. He waved the chunk of meat on his fork to emphasize his point. He chewed, swallowed, and then pointed at us with his knife. "What's been your favorite city on this trip?"

"Barcelona," Lucy replied.

"Yes, I agree," I said. "Amsterdam was fun. Hey, it was a lot of fun. But Barcelona is a true party town."

"Plus you got laid there."

"Yes, I did. Another notch on my bedpost."

"That's one less than me." Ben was keeping score.

"One less? You've had two encounters?"

"Well, if we'd stop going to gay clubs, maybe I could be part of this conversation," Lucy said, shaking her head while stirring her gravy.

"I know we both got laid in Amsterdam, Ben, but where else did you get laid?" I asked.

"I got laid twice in Amsterdam," he replied. "You see, there was one night I couldn't sleep and..."

"Do you guys ever give it a rest?" Lucy asked.

"Do we really need to answer that?" I replied. "So, Ben, where did you find him?"

He panted like a puppy. "All I'll say is, a leather club opened my eyes."

"You went to the leather club without me?"

"Yeah," said Lucy. "You went to the leather club without us?"

"Well, when a boy wants to play hard, you know, friends are better left behind. Besides, you two were asleep."

"How do you know? Did you check on us?"

"Of course not. What if you were awake?"

I raised my wine glass. "To my favorite slutty workmate and friend." My buddies also raised their glasses. "And to you too, Lucy, who gets plenty of sex back home in Sydney."

She grinned wickedly.

"You could have got laid in Berlin," said Ben.

"True," I added. "There was an experience I'm sure you'd never get offered back home."

"No way! That pierced guy was freaky."

"But he wanted you."

"Yeah, but for what?

"He had more holes than a target at a shooting range," Ben added.

Even lilac lady laughed. We downed our drinks before she brought another bottle.

"Just think," said Lucy. "Tomorrow we're traveling home."

"Don't talk about it," I replied. "I don't want this holiday to end."

"I'm glad we're finishing our trip in a cheap country," Ben added. "My credit card is maxed out."

"Me too."

"Me three," said Lucy.

"I don't know why you're complaining. You own the café we work in, boss. You make all the money. I'm dreading seeing my bank statement."

"Now, now, Nathan. I promised I'd get Ben to teach you how to make coffee. I need another barista. It pays better than being a waiter."

I half smiled.

"And I know you're just as fussy about coffee as I am," Ben declared. "You'll have those office workers lining up for their morning hit of caffeine. You'll be a great pusher."

"Pusher?" I asked.

"Yeah. Their addiction and your will to supply an aromatic brew of premium roasted liquid dependence will make you a top-class dealer."

"He's right," said Lucy. "Morning coffee is what keeps my café afloat."

"I just have to get used to being a morning person," I admitted. "But still, it's a sacrifice I'm prepared to make for better pay." I refilled our glasses and raised mine. "A toast to a wonderful couple of friends and a wonderful three weeks away from work!"

"Yay, Europe," said Ben. "Well, at least the little we've seen of it." He clinked my glass.

"I'll drink to that." Lucy swirled her wine before she drank. "And you guys have been great travel companions."

"Thank you, boss."

"And will you two stop calling me boss? I'd like to think I'm more to you than that."

"You are, boss."

She stared at Ben with murderous eyes. "Do you enjoy working at the café?"

"You can't fire me. I have to teach Nathan how to make coffee."

"You're right. I'll wait until after you teach him." She poked her tongue out.

"So, shall we do the same thing next year?" I asked. "Maybe South America? Or shall we keep the cost down and discover Asia?" I sipped. "What about...?"

"Did you run out of battery power?" Lucy asked.

"What are you looking at?" Ben queried. He turned to see what made me pause midsentence.

The culprit stood at the entrance of the restaurant. Shortly cropped dark hair. Rosy lips curved as if a sculptor had created them by smoothing their surface with the tip of his finger. His stylishly knitted red sweater hung loosely, making his upper body a mystery. And his thick black-rimmed glasses had me picturing him on my couch, reading quietly before I'd slowly pull them off his face, exposing my own superhero.

"Nathan, are you home?" Lucy asked.

The man saw me, smiled, and then made his way to the closest empty table.

"Are you dining alone?" Ben called out to him.

I gulped my wine, nearly spilling some on my food. Then I choked. My dream man rushed over. Lucy pounded me hard on my upper back. I felt like a slab of steak getting tenderized. He gave me a glass of water. I took it, drinking steadily.

"Are you okay?" he said in an American accent.

"Yes," I whispered through strained vocal cords. "Thanks for the water."

"My pleasure." He gazed at me, mystic eyes behind dark frames.

"His name is Nathan," said my boss. "And I'm Lucy. And this is Ben."

"I'm Cameron." We all shook hands before he pulled up a chair. "What's with this violin music?"

"See that lilac-clad waitress?" Ben replied. "It's her son's music she's boring us with."

We all stared in her direction. She waved cheerfully before fishing around for an extra glass. She brought it over. Ben poured the wine.

"So why are you dining alone?" I finally found the courage to speak.

"Time away to clear my head."

"From what?"

"My family. Sometimes I just need a break from them."

"So, you came to Prague?"

"It's a bit of a distance, I know, but I wanted a place I could daydream in. And a friend suggested Prague."

"Good choice," said Lucy.

"Are you going anywhere else after Prague?" I asked.

"I don't know. I've had some suggestions from the backpackers at my hostel, but I'm open to ideas."

"Well, we're just ending our short trip. We've been to Barcelona, Berlin, Paris, Amsterdam, and now here."

"Have you got plans for tonight, Cameron?" Lucy asked.

"Not at the moment, no." His eyes wandered in my direction as he spoke.

Ben raised his hand to get lilac lady's attention. "Bill, please."

"Don't you mean check?"

"You say tom-ay-to, we say tom-ah-to," replied Ben.

"You say bell pepper, we say capsicum," Lucy added.

"You say duvet, we say doona," I said. "And the list goes on and on."

"I see," he replied. "We say check, you say bill. Got it. But do you need to go so soon?"

Lucy pointed at me. "Oh, he's staying here. Ben and I need to go and…" She searched thin air for the end of her sentence.

"We need to go and find somewhere to do our laundry," Ben continued. "It's been a long trip."

"At this hour?"

"Hey, there's a river up the road. We can wash our underwear in the water."

"But you haven't finished your dinner."

"We're full," said Lucy unconvincingly.

My friends stood, made their way to the waitress, and paid for our meals. As they left, Lucy blew me a kiss.

"I recommend the goulash, Cameron. It's really good."

"Can I taste yours?"

I fed his curvy lips. He chewed slowly, never taking his eyes off me. "What do you think?"

"I think you're almost done, Nathan, and you'd be watching me eat if I ordered now."

Lilac woman brought over a small plate of the local stew, then picked up the wine bottle and refilled our glasses. We thanked her as she smiled kindly.

"You've got no choice now," I said.

We clinked glasses.

"I guess that makes it official," he said.

"You guess this makes what official?"

"I'm on a date with a charismatic guy called Nathan."